I0610622

CONFLICT
OF INTEREST

LORI HUGHES

Hughes, Lori, author
Conflict of Interest/Lori Hughes

ISBN (pbk): 978-0-9938196-4-3
ISBN (ebook): 978-0-9938196-5-0

Design by OneBigMachine.com

Sexcess.org
info@sexcess.org

Sexcess.org is a division of
YAANTM Inc.
2704-628 Fleet Street
Toronto, ON
M5V 1A8

Author's note

The only thing I like to do more than read is write … but I love them both. Maybe equally? And I love to write, equally, about love and sex because one without the other is not reality. Ironically, we find the reality of our human sexuality and our most basic needs in fiction. That's why I write about people in quest of unadulterated sexual passion, the archway to unbridled love. It's a wild, wicked and wonderful journey through life.

I am glad you can join the journey.

Lori Hughes

A QUICK PEEK INSIDE TO KINDLE YOUR FANTASY

There was no thought, just need. She wanted to let go. But couldn't. She had to be in charge, not give into his sexual magnetism. She slid a hand between them and forced him, hard, against the back of the sofa. She whispered, "I'm in charge."

Private jets were not new to her but this … *OMG*. The interior was custom-designed to somebody's very particular taste. His. The cabin was decorated in a palette of fawn-colored leather, dark rich wood and stainless-steel trim and in addition to eight plush seats there was a beautiful sofa opposite a slim cabinet with a TV and fresh flowers on it. She hoped the flowers were standard accessories, not a romantic suggestion. The sofa triggered her sexual fantasies and clouded her decision as to where to sit. His hand touched the small of her back.

The meeting was getting heated. He asked. "Victoria, do you not see the imperative here?"

She didn't. Other than the imperative to sexually devour him. "No. I see an acquisition stalled because of the need for critical paperwork. And – "

"Fuck." He hit the table with his hand.

She had fantasized about that hand many a night.

And whenever he said 'fuck,' she instinctively wanted to shout, *yes!*

When he'd first met her his immediate thought was, *stunning* – and surprisingly young for such high achievement. Elegantly sexy, she was engaging. Captivating. And there was a calm knowing in her bluest of blue eyes. She exuded an all-business, take-no-crap persona, and carried herself with an arms-length coolness that increased the fascination. He'd done business with brilliant minds, and pleasure with beautiful women, but she was both.

The exhilaration was consuming. His brawn had always sent ripples of urgency through her but here, on his yacht, in the rising sun and stiffening breeze, his height and thickness pictured against the waves was what she imagined Ulysses and legendary seafarers must have looked like. Straining body, intense mind, surging muscles, all running against the sea. She could not escape the seductive forces, strengthening like the wind, willing her toward freedom.

LOVE & SEXCESS™

'Once upon a time' lasts forever, and we create stories of unabashed romance and intriguing mystery to nourish your unadulterated desires and seduce your limitless imagination.

If you like *Conflict of Interest*, try *Deadsizing* and *Sacred Corruption*, plus our monthly short stories and serial novellas.

Visit: **Sexcess.org**

CHAPTER ONE

Victoria crossed the expansive boardroom, trying to suppress the rhythm of her heart, the rise in her breathing and the stirring of her femininity. The unwavering eyes of Yale Walters drew her in, almost willing her over the Persian carpet. He shook her hand, placed his other hand on top of hers and said something. She said something. She heard nothing. But his eyes said everything. And her inner-spirit danced across every erogenous nerve-ending of her body.

This was a repeat performance, a recurring dilemma every time they met. She'd met many wealthy investors, powerful CEOs and egomaniacs, all legends in their own mind, so last week when her boss, Carl Kennor, Chairman of Kennor Capital, had invited her to a meeting she had no expectations. He'd said, 'Yale Walters is brash, brilliant, a born winner and charming as hell.' He was definitely brash. And brilliant. And a winner – as far as she could tell. But charming didn't come close to describing him and drop-dead gorgeous was an inadequate cliché. He was tall, six-two … three. Lean. Athletic. His taut chest and shoulders always looked like they wanted to escape his custom-tailored suit, and his thick, dark hair and firm-edged jaw framed the most intriguing smile she'd ever encountered. And his eyes were like warm pools of deep brown, maple syrup, sweet, and yet dangerous to a woman's health. Since they first met, the sexual tension in their 'strictly-business' relationship has been, for her, *one helluva conflict of interest.*

He took a seat at the table. "Victoria, I was just telling Carl about our pending problem."

Our problem? Or your problem? His eyes held her as if she was the only person in the room. She looked away, nodded at her boss and gathered her thoughts. "Carl filled me in. You need the first $100 million tomorrow. But we still need your personal disclosure forms before we transfer funds." She stood on the opposite side of the table and exhaled slowly, trying to sound cool and detached, despite her swelling heat.

He didn't miss a beat. "You both know this is a one-time opportunity." He looked at Carl, then her, eyes penetrating, sensing her rising pulse. "But we have to move quickly."

Carl said, "It's up to Victoria. It's her project."

She tamped down her erotic response as he explained to Carl the urgency of closing the half-billion-dollar deal. She watched. When he was intense, she saw sexual prowess; when he was calm she saw sexual sensitivity. For her, everything was visceral – and a problem. She was a clear-thinking, tough-minded investment manager and he was just another client ... except he wasn't. Since they'd first met, he was the source of sexual fantasies like she'd never had before, and struggled to control.

She worked with good-looking, powerful men all the time – admittedly, none as potent – and sexual tension was to be expected, as long as it didn't get in the way of the only emotion that mattered, the love of money. She had in the past, indulged in flirting, some dating, and unattached sex. But this? She couldn't explain it. Or deny it. Or control it. But she must. Because in the investment business there was a Biblical rule; money rules, not emotions. Sex, yes; anything more, forbidden. And with Kennor Capital investing $400 million in Yale's acquisition, he was off limits, out of bounds ... forbidden. Relegated to fantasy.

During their meetings, his brashness and brilliance were on full display and as they'd worked on the deal she'd been able, so far, to manage her flights of sexual fantasy. Like now, as he made the case to Carl, she watched every movement. Eyes, hands, standing, sitting, leaning, stretching, frowning, smiling … hard questions, soft words. He was convincing, confident … and all consuming. As always, she was moved. And moist.

He asked. "Victoria, do you not see the imperative here?"

She didn't. Other than the imperative to sexually devour him. "No. I see an acquisition stalled because of the need for critical paperwork. And – "

"Fuck." He hit the table with his hand.

She'd fantasized about that hand many a night. And whenever he said 'fuck,' she instinctively wanted to shout, *yes!*

His eyes went black. "What the fuck is it with paperwork, paperwork, paperwork?"

She saw the plea. Had seen it before in clients. All demanding and urgent until they realized who controlled the money. She did. And it was her leverage over him, she was in charge. *The image distracted her.* She might be in charge, but she wasn't in control. She said, "Whenever you're available, I'm ready to get the documentation done."

He rose to his feet. "How about tonight, my office – seven?"

As he stood, her mind stood still. He seemed even taller and thicker, rising above her like an athlete on a podium, a winner – strong, confident, victorious. A hunk of sexual pleasure. From the midst of her distraction she shot a reply. "Seven works."

"See you then." He shook Carl's hand, then hers.

His handshake was different. Everything about him was different.

• • •

The security guard stared at her lecherously as she signed in. "Thirty-seventh floor Ma'am."

She reminded herself, *this is just another meeting.* Carl had said Yale was seldom on the ground more than a day or two as he crisscrossed countries and oceans like most people commute to the office, and his office was usually on his private jet, thirty thousand feet in the air. Tonight, he was on the ground in New York.

She was glad the elevator was unoccupied, it gave her a minute to steady her emotions. She couldn't decipher between nervousness and excitement, but most of it was excitement because she was good at dealing with nervousness. It was part of the survival kit in her line of work. But this excitement was different. This man had her stirring where business isn't supposed to be. *I never should have rushed home to change. Now I'm overdressed. It's the diamond and pearl drop pendant, it's too much.*

She'd shuffled another client and canceled a meeting to accommodate his seven o'clock request, and then at six o'clock jumped in a cab and rushed home to change. She'd always been self-conscious about how she looked. Everyone thought it was vanity, but she knew it was insecurity. She cleared her throat – a childhood nervous habit – and thought, *how ironic, it's he who should be nervous, not me. He needs me.* Tomorrow she would recommend, yes or no, on whether Kennor Capital, would invest $400 million, along with a $100 million from his company, Apogee Holdings, to acquire the high-tech company, Xcryption Inc.

But all the millions and all the logic didn't change her reality, a reality she'd experienced only once before – unprompted, raw attraction that was more than just lust. Could she stay objective and suppress the emotions? And why did she go home to change from a perfectly good, beige suit into a coral jacket, black Armani skirt, silk blouse and drop pendent – and black lingerie? *Just because they're my favorites?*

Before the elevator opened she smoothed the front of her skirt, re-buttoned her jacket, acknowledged her reflection in the steel doors and summoned a ton of self-restraint.

The receptionist greeted her. "Hello Ms. Dyson. I'll let Mr.

Walters know you're here."

She didn't bother to sit. She didn't want to suggest she expected to wait. As a woman, it was a tactic she used when competing in the male-dominated, power-world, high above the glass ceiling. She dealt with CEOs and Wall Street sharks and never let them intimidate her. There were only two outward signs of her inner anxiety. One, she couldn't control a periodic clearing of her throat and two, after a pressure-packed day, she'd go home and indulge in peanut butter. Not a sandwich, right out of the jar, by the spoonful. She'd downed five dollops before coming to this meeting.

Yale was on edge – it was Victoria. And she'd just arrived. He'd missed his workout and felt it – not irritation or anger, just edge. Thirty minutes on the treadmill would have helped. And he still had to talk to the Pentagon about signing the contract, which they wouldn't do until Victoria committed the funds. He was confident she would, but securing $400 million was never a slam-dunk, even for him. He needed Kennor Capital's first check for $100 million in Apogee's bank account, tomorrow. It was up to her.

When he'd first met her his immediate thought was, *stunning* – and surprisingly young for such high achievement. He soon learned how self-assured, knowledgeable and razor-sharp she was, operating independently of her boss, and neither an ass-kisser or a hard-ass. Although she sure had a great ass. Attractive in the way tall, svelte model-types are defined, with classic high cheekbones framed by thick, naturally blonde hair, cut short. Elegantly sexy, she was engaging. Captivating. And there was a calm knowing in her bluest of blue eyes. She exuded an all-business, take-no-crap persona, like a serious financial manager should, and carried herself with an arms-length coolness that increased the fascination. But behind the beauty there was something he couldn't quite discern. Yes, a young woman of beauty and intellect, but there was an emotional apprehension – maybe about him? Her eyes radiated a fascination, but her body language revealed a fight against that fascination. He was familiar with women's vulnerability, but not with anyone this poised and intriguing. He'd done business with brilliant minds and pleasure with beautiful women, but she was both. That meant there'd be an extra benefit in it for him if he had to make a physical investment in her assets – her unlawfully sexual beauty – if it was necessary in securing her financial investment in his asset.

"Ms. Dyson, Mr. Walters is running behind … a few more minutes." The receptionist was apologetic, but it gave her time to refocus on the business at hand – money. Big money.

Then he was there, striding through the door, his smile full of promise. "Sorry Victoria … come in, come in."

"I'm sure you're backed-up."

"You look great." He touched her arm, guiding her to his office and opening the door into its ultra-modern, stainless steel and glass décor with soaring windows. His expansive desk and matching boardroom table were only overshadowed by a grand piano in the corner. The view of Central Park was spectacular. She stepped ahead of him, needing the space to subdue the blood rush.

After an hour of reviewing financials, she was finished with her questions. He had a superb grasp of the business and was full of confidence but, paradoxically, it led to one of his weaknesses – lack of documentation. That drove her nuts. When it came to money, she wanted every "t" crossed and "i" dotted. For him, it was much to do about nothing.

At one point, when he didn't have information at hand he'd said, "Victoria, you have to trust me." That was her fear. Her dilemma. She wanted to trust him – had to – but couldn't. And she didn't trust her own vacillating feelings about him, from primitive want, to intuitive distrust. She had to get rid of one and hold fast to the other because with her ruthless boss there was no room for error – either this guy delivers returns, or else. She looked at the grandfather clock. "Enough for tonight."

He stood up. "Let's celebrate. Something to eat?"

"I'll grab something at home." *Why the hell did I say that?*

"Nonsense. I've got dinner – went to great expense." He smiled and winked.

Bet he can do a lot of things at the same time.

"Chinese take-out. Peking duck?

"Love it."

"I have a special Chardonnay."

He touched the phone. "Taylor, well take dinner now."

His assistant set out linen napkins, placemats and wine glasses on the table. It was elegant, until Taylor set the cardboard containers down. He opened the Chardonnay – she knew wines, it was Kistler, from Napa Valley, about a hundred-dollars a bottle.

"Chopsticks?"

"Fork. I'm a klutz."

"Can't imagine you being a klutz at anything."

"You'd be surprised."

"Tell me something you're a klutz at."

"Some things should always be secret. My klutziness is one of them." *All the rest I'm ready to reveal to you, whenever you want.*

"Now you've got me intrigued. Agree, secrets are to be kept, but it's fun to uncover them. Let me guess."

They were playing. She liked it. "One guess."

"This is dangerous. One wrong guess and I could be in big trouble. But I'll risk it." He leaned back in his chair, eyes scanning her as if she was naked in an MRI machine. "If you're a klutz with chopsticks, you're probably … I can't believe those beautiful fingers are klutzy at anything but … if you're hands lack dexterity with small things, like nuts and bolts, then maybe – "

"What? You don't think I'm a nuts and bolts kinda gal? Who likes digging into details and – "

"No, no. Didn't mean that. Meant mechanical. Like picking up teeny-weeny nuts. You know?" He rubbed his fingers together pretending there were little nuts on the table. "Like in a toolbox."

Her mind was already in the wrong place, racing with sexual innuendos and dirty thoughts. *I might not be good with teeny-weeny nuts, but sure love to reach out and pick up your bag of beautiful nuts. And those gorgeous long fingers could be in my toolbox anytime.* "You're right, I'm a klutz when it comes to tools – hammers, nails, screwdrivers, screws ..." *stop before you say something crude.*

"So, I guessed right. I win." He went to his desk. "Is there a prize?" He clicked a key on his computer and the venetian blinds, stretching across the floor-to-ceiling glass wall, closed. The outer office disappeared. They were alone.

The mood shifted from all business to all-relaxed.

He said, "You know what I forgot? I never found those contracts you wanted." He went to a pile of documents on the coffee table.

"Later," she said. "Send them in the morning." She didn't want to go back to business. For the last few minutes her feelings had run in the other direction and she didn't want them to stop. They were vivid – and dirty – but under control, pulsating between her mind and her core.

He was engrossed in his search. "Gotta find 'em … or never will. And that wouldn't please my nuts and bolts partner."

Fighting self-control, she moved to the sofa next to the coffee table. She marveled at him. Behind his intensity was commitment; behind his charm, a zest for life; behind his knowledge, a ravenous intellect. And behind it all, a rebel streak, a maverick – a high risk, don't-give-a-damn, adventure-seeking guy. She didn't doubt that part of him would rather be in jeans and chaps, trying to tame a wild bronco instead of wearing custom-tailored suits and trying to persuade investment bankers – even attractive females. *I'd love to be his bucking bronco.*

Sitting on the sofa as he rummaged, she chuckled, and he gave her a don't-make-fun-of-me look. She was enthralled, absorbing every inch of his energy. Then she set her wine glass down, moved next to him and started going through a stack of files. She didn't give a damn about the files, just followed her urge to be closer. The search was beginning to frustrate him, and he didn't notice how he brushed against her when he moved. She noticed. Her heat was rising, mouth drying, inner thighs warming. She had to separate. She kicked off her heels and moved to the corner of the sofa. The space helped, a little.

"Got it." He triumphantly held up a wad of papers.

"Great," she said. "Now that's the end of work."

He grinned like a kid who had just caught his first fish. It reminded her of a boy she had a crush on when she was seventeen. His name was Alan. He wasn't much of a catch, but he loved to fish and one day caught a big catfish and gave it to her. She hated fish. But not boys. Back then she wasn't much of a catch, so she rewarded Alan by giving him her virginity. But she really was a tomboy, not a prom-queen. Long, gangly legs and nicknamed "Skinny Minnie." She wasn't unpopular, just ordinary. So she dated a little and studied a lot. By the time she was in university her beauty, as her father said, had 'blossomed,' which was confirmed by most guys declaring her the 'hottest Theta' in the Kappa Alpha Theta sorority. But despite a waiting list of overheated dates, she was in love with learning and driven to be independent.

He went to the kitchenette. "More wine?"

He poured the Chardonnay and then did what he shouldn't have. Sat next to her and stretched his long, sexy legs across the coffee table. All of him, on full display, within arms-length. *I could reach over and touch his cock without even spilling my wine … control yourself girl.*

He was soon reminiscing about his days at Stanford and how he'd always planned to have his own business. He said his plans went on hold for a few years before focusing on what was now Apogee Holdings.

"Why on hold?"

He glanced at her. The answer was there, but he didn't offer it. The pull was intense. "I know what your resume says, Hewlett-Packard, SpaceX – some day you must tell me about Elon Musk. But that's not putting things on hold."

"HP and SpaceX were good years, no regrets. Learned to fly."

She couldn't deny her need. She touched his arm. "But why on hold?" She got an unexpected response. She wasn't sure if it was to her question or her touch. And didn't care. He laid his hand on hers, mesmerizing eyes pulling her in. His grip was firm.

"I got tangled up in a problem – unintended – that tied me up, damn near strangled me. Was involved with a lawyer – a woman – who got me into a deal that had a huge upside. It seemed so good I never questioned her due diligence – the lack of." He grimaced. "We did the deal, but when I dug further, didn't like what I saw. But it was too late. I was in. We were partners. The company had great value but it, and her, didn't reflect my values." He grimaced. "I sold my shares and fired her. We wanted the same thing, wealth, but came from different worlds, and had different ideas about how to get it. She came from money – with expectations and questionable practices. But I didn't see her for who she really was." He shrugged. "In the end, it worked out because it's through her that I got this chance to buy the company, Xcryption, back. With the help of your $400 million."

For the first time, she saw vulnerability. *Was it the woman?* She risked the next question not sure she wanted the answer. She squeezed his arm "You said partners. As in married?"

"Hell no. My only marriage is to this insufferable company." He shifted closer. "I'm a monogamous man, and the company gets all my attention. Make quite the couple … you think?"

"Odd couple."

"I need her, she needs me. Has to be – "

"Do you believe all work and no play makes Yale a dull boy?"

He laughed. And stroked her arm. "You think I'm dull?"

If you stroke my arm again, I'll suck every ounce of dullness out of you. "Not at all, I just – "

"Bored with me?"

She placed her other hand on top of his and an inner voice said, *don't!* Her voice started from somewhere beyond her dirty thoughts and sounded too sultry. "I've never been bored, not for a moment. We're going to be working together, very closely" ... *that was too suggestive.* She uncurled her legs and nestled against him.

Domination crept into his eyes. Without a word, he slipped an arm around her waist, pulled her into his chest. He pressed his leg against hers and held her for a long moment.

Nuzzled against his rugged torso, she slipped into the scent of his skin. It was so natural and as he drew his head back, her mouth searched upward. He took it. There was no thought, just need.

She wanted to let herself go. But couldn't. She had to be in charge, not give into his sexual magnetism. She slid a hand between them and forced him, hard, against the back of the sofa. She whispered, "I'm in charge." He sank submissively into the cushions as she pulled up her skirt and straddled him. She pressed into his groin, forcing her heat against his erection and he grabbed her shoulders, crushing his lips into hers. Tongues penetrated and a commanding hand slipped between her thighs, possessing her wetness. Sexual desperation mounted as his fingers eased inside her panties, opening her swollen desire.

Then her mouth pulled away. Her heat receded, and she rose above him, escaping his fingers, lifting away ...

He opened his eyes. A gasp of raging need rushed out. "What the ...?"

"I ... I ... I mustn't ... stupid. *I'm* stupid. I never.... What the hell am I thinking?" Between pursed lips, she was berating herself, colliding emotions swelling in her temples. She stood up and pushed her skirt down. It was as if she'd just been ripped from a bad dream, having saved herself from plummeting off a cliff into a whirlpool of ecstasy. She was trying to compose herself, while still staring at the straining heat in his pants. The shock was severe, the disappointment wrenching, the anger suppressed … But control was imperative.

"Victoria? What the – ?"

She blurted. "Fuck." And turned away, crossing the room, running fingers through her hair and quelling her still boiling heat. She stopped in front of the windows, staring into the darkness. "Fuck!"

"You can say that again," he exclaimed and sat up.

She turned to face him. He didn't seem ruffled. "Yale, I'm sorry … My fault. Never should've happened. Won't happen again…. I look forward to being your business partner, nothing more."

"I think – "

She raised her hand. "Stop."

He said. "It's okay, we can keep things separate, don't have to – "

"There's no room for this," she said. But couldn't avoid his gaze. Hot. Demanding. Still hungry. She turned back to the windows and spoke into the blackness hanging over Central Park. "This was a mistake." But she heard her inner resentment. *I fucking want him. Badly. Why can't we just fuck and be done with it.* This was not about business. This was a long way from business. Someplace she liked very much – and so did he. Until something clicked inside her. Something about him, something warning her to proceed with caution. Yes, she'd almost surrendered to his sexually magnificent body, but he hadn't resisted either. She'd seen a shift in his eyes, a knowing, a glint, an anticipation of … victory. Was this all business for him, including the sex? All for the love of money? The doubt was maybe what stopped her? Zapped her carnal craving and allowed her to regain control. She sure as hell wanted him but proved she could resist him. She took a deep breath, "We both wanted this. And we know we can't."

He stood up. "Understood." He looked cool. Felt cool. "No need for this to be a problem. We can play it anyway you want."

Play it? You think this is a game? She repressed her rising heat, anger mixing with need.

"Just as long as there are no problems between us." He went to the kitchenette for a bottle of water. "This is business. That's it! Money, technology, focus. You're a financial whiz, a brilliant woman, a source of money. That's what I need … this is just a delightful side benefit. A dividend payment." He smiled.

She knew detachment when she saw it. But he'd certainly penetrated her protective edge, opening up something that was frighteningly real. And risky. She had reached past his well-honed persona, but was uncertain if this was all just 'playing it' the way he wanted?

He was back to all-business and whatever they'd shared was gone. *Maybe for the best? But it sure as hell didn't feel that way.* One thing was certain, the conflict of interest wasn't gone.

After diversionary small talk, she closed her briefcase, put on her jacket and prepared to leave. It was as if she was leaving a funeral. He walked her to reception and shook her hand. She couldn't not touch him, just a hand on the arm. "We were both wrong."

"Good-night Victoria." His eyes said something else.

CHAPTER TWO

The next morning Victoria made a strong recommendation to invest, but it was followed by a disappointing, one-way conversation with Carl Kennor. She was blindsided. In no uncertain terms, he stuck his big nose in her personal life and spoke bluntly.

"If you sleep with Walters, you're off the project."

He couldn't possibly know about last night.

He explained that the attraction between them was obvious and he considered the risk too great, characterizing it as emotional weakness. Then he tried to sound fatherly and exhibit a modicum of care. He said, "Normally, I don't give a damn about who fucks who, but I consider you, Victoria, special. And he's too dangerous. I don't want to lose you, or this deal, because of emotional entanglement."

She read between the lines. It was the deal that mattered, not her.

She was depressed. So she did what she always did and ate from a stash of peanut butter in her desk, and then went shopping – at least Saks and American Express would like her.

Kennor Capital put up the first $100 million and in less than a week a second $100 million was due, but she still hadn't received Yale's personal disclosure documentation and was trying to track him down.

She walked into Carl's office. "He's impossible. Never available. Never returns my calls. *You* try and get him."

"I did," said Carl. "But you're responsible for this project *and* him – not me."

She dropped like an overburdened camel into the sumptuous

leather of Kennor's sofa and allowed all her female independence to slouch. She was tired, frazzled, frustrated. But she wasn't about to be beaten. This venture would succeed, despite Yale's lack of attention to details. And her sexual attraction to him would just be a footnote, not a factor. But today was more than a bad hair day, even though her hair did need a cut. Here she was trying to get some help from her boss and he was just offering more pressure.

Carl walked around his desk and sat on the front edge. "We've got a big investment in this guy, but there's something in his background he's not disclosing." His tone was unmistakable. "Find out what the hell's going on. The upside is tremendous, the downside not pretty. If this goes bad, we're in trouble."

The 'we,' meant her, no one else. She knew the rules – high risk, high reward, no sympathy. She'd been with Kennor for three years and recognized that her boss, despite a shortage of social graces, was long on investment savvy. The success of his multi-billion-dollar firm was because he was brilliant, blunt, tough and connected to everyone. Their mutual respect, plus the large amount of money he paid her, was why she'd stuck it out. She was a rising star, the youngest portfolio manager in the firm and, although he never said it, his protégé. If the investment with Yale paid off, she'd become one of the top money makers at the firm. And rich. Not Kennor-rich, or Yale-rich, but certainly Victoria-rich. She was driven to find her pot of gold at the south end of Manhattan, not for the glitz and glamor but for the freedom it provided. Her late father used to say 'independence' was her middle name. Except, right now she was much too dependent on one beguiling man.

Carl's secretary stepped in. "Mr. Walters on line three, sir."

"That's for you Victoria. Looks like he's quick to return *my* call." His smile was intended to soften the point.

She reached for the phone, removing her earring and pushing the irritation aside. Her back straightened and her professional skills clicked in. "Yale. Thanks for calling back." At times he made her want to scream and his unavailability was exasperating. He was her Jekyll and Hyde, constantly inflaming conflicts within her. She now compartmentalized her attraction to him and labeled it respect, but didn't respect the way he was ignoring her.

He was furious. He had to get Xcryption's Pentagon contract signed and deposit the next hundred-million so the current owner couldn't back out, but without the paperwork, she wasn't releasing the next payment.

She held the phone away from her ear so Kennor could hear.

He said. "In Boston. Wheels up in ten minutes. Only one thing I need to know. Have you transferred the funds?"

"Not yet – "

"What's the fuckin' problem?"

She ignored her visceral reaction.

He said, "You're jeopardizing the deal. Without the second payment, this could – "

"Slow down" she said. "You're forgetting something." She was calm but assertive. Part of her wanted to hang up. She hated these confrontations. He made her head and core ache, all at the same time. She wasn't in the mood. Besides, he was wrong. Jetting off to Boston this morning, claiming he didn't have time for her requests but needed the money. Well, she needed the paperwork, including his personal information – background and medical. He'd undermined her trust, financially and personally. *No more.* Fortunately – unfortunately for him – she was in charge. She stifled an erotic image.

"This conversation will get us nowhere. Call me when you're back."

"Noon."

"Fine."

He was gone.

She dropped the phone in its cradle. Something between frustration and exhaustion pushed the smile from her face, *he's going to be the death of me.*

• • •

Yale sipped the wine and tried to enjoy the smoked salmon being served on his Gulfstream G600. He only had a few days before the deal had to close and he needed money, not blow back. *Damn her.*

"More wine sir? ... Excuse me sir, more wine?"

Deep in thought, he turned from the vastness outside the window and nodded. He glanced at the svelte stewardess as she walked back to the galley. *Nice ... sexy. But nothing compared to Victoria. Not even close. Damn her.*

He checked his schedule. New York this afternoon, to Washington this evening and a late dinner, meetings tomorrow morning and then off to the conference in Grenada. *I'm not up for dinner with Zofia tonight. But have to go.* Zofia Gorka was a ghost from the past and now, a necessary evil. She was his ex-lawyer and the woman who had originally brought him into what is now Xcyrption. A few years ago, she'd overseen his investment in the company, which was controlled by her father, J. K Kondracki (a.k.a. JK). Later he discovered that JK was a man of reprehensible character and an arms dealer. Now, in an effort to take over the business, he was attempting to buyout JK for half-a-billion. All was going well until JK found another buyer, a third-world country offering $800 million. But he couldn't get out once Yale had paid the $200 million – coming from Victoria. Due by the end of the week. JK was determined to stop the deal and would go to any lengths. Zofia knew JK's secrets and where the skeletons were buried, which is why she was critical to his plan, even though she was the last person he wanted to get involved with.

Their relationship had been more than business, as it was with many of the beautiful women he worked with, and they were all clear on the purpose – unadulterated pleasure, nothing more. No attachments. Which is why the aborted encounter with Victoria last night was probably a good thing. Even though she'd set off alarm bells in his head, he hadn't heard them because he couldn't ignore what she did to his body. She made every fiber of his being shudder. But he could handle a sexual relationship if it would lead to closing this deal.

He frowned into the vastness outside his jet. It was cloudy, like the future. A future that must be protected from his past, and a past that must be protected from Victoria. He would meet Zofia tonight in D.C., and as far as Victoria was concerned, he'd do whatever was necessary, including fulfill her fantasies, if required.

It was just after noon when he threw his jacket on the chair and called her.

"Victoria ... Yale."

"How was the flight?"

He didn't need polite; he needed money. "I'm running late on some overseas calls."

She was pointed. "Here's what I need – "

He retorted. "Let's talk about what *I* need, what the company needs. The next hundred million. It's that simple. No check, no deal. No deal, no contract. No contract, no company – no return on your investment." He paused. "Not a pretty picture."

I hate fighting him. He'd ignored her requests, assuming when the crunch came she'd put up the money. A typical entrepreneur, a high-flying swashbuckler. He just assumed she'd come through because if she didn't it would mean the loss of the hundred-million already invested. His 'not a pretty picture' comment was a not-too-veiled threat. But she was about to change the rules of the game.

"Yale." Her tone was controlled. "The reason the picture isn't pretty is because Apogee has violated the terms of our agreement. Put Kennor Capital in a difficult spot. We're in a legal position to hold back funds. If the deal to buy Xcryption doesn't happen, Kennor will sue Apogee ... and you." She paused. "You're right, not a pretty picture."

"Sue me? You're kidding? Carl wouldn't do that. You certainly wouldn't – "

She reminded herself, *he's just another investment risk*. Except she couldn't forget the sexual energy in this 'investment risk,' the energy that almost exploded last night in his office. Pushing aside the involuntary erotic zap, she said, "Don't bet on it. And Apogee doesn't have enough money to bet. Kennor does. We'd rather write-off a hundred now versus throw in another hundred and write-off two. You do the math."

He couldn't let stupid paperwork and a tough-assed Victoria sabotage everything he'd worked for. She didn't know what was at stake. She was just the keeper of the money. First, he had to get the money, then worry about the rest. She was one controlling bitch, but he'd seen her vulnerability. "Victoria, look … I don't mean to be difficult, but we know each other, nothing personal should distract from the money. Nothing." He paused. "We can resolve this."

She flushed. She really didn't know him, but wanted to – all of him. "It will be resolved." She imagined him smiling as he heard her declaration. *Don't smile, you haven't heard the new rules.* "I've reviewed everything with Carl." She hadn't, and didn't need to, but wanted to make sure he didn't do an end-run and call Carl after he heard what she was about to tell him. "In order to receive the next hundred million, we're making some changes. Which I'm sure you won't like." She coughed to clear the icky taste in her throat. "But I'll be clear. There's no compromise. You accept the terms or no money. Kennor will sever all ties and start legal proceedings." She got only silence – either shock or anger. She visualized his face on full-alert; lips pressed, jaw tilted, eyes crunched – fiercely intense, heatedly handsome, seriously sexy. Her mind and body slipped back into the near-climatic event on his couch. She choked off the feelings, *it's just business.*

"I've drawn up a letter. It sets out new terms under which

Kennor Captial is prepared to release the next hundred. Let me – ”

"Wait, wait. I don't know what's in your letter, but you can't change the rules now. We're on the verge of finalizing the deal and you're playing brinkmanship. What the hell – ”

"It's straightforward." She said it but didn't believe anything would ever again be straightforward between them. "When you read the letter, you'll see that until you provide the requested paperwork, and after we acquire Xcryption, I'll be Chief Financial Officer and Board Chair … you'll remain CEO." The next words stuck, then she spit them out. "… reporting to me."

"What – ?"

"We're protecting our investment. Pure and simple – ”

"*I* report to *you*? What the fuck?"

She heard the inner, *yes*. But said, "I'm making sure what has to happen, happens. Once I'm satisfied … *if that's even possible? …* I'll relinquish the two positions." She was afraid to slow down. "As soon as you sign the letter, I'll transfer the hundred million. Then we'll go over getting the rest of the paperwork done and how we work together."

Her words pounded inside his head. He fought the anger. *Report to her?* She had no idea the implications. Or how, on the threshold of success, she was putting everything at risk. "Victoria," he tried to sound non-confrontational. "Email the letter. Then I'll call you back."

"I'll send it for your perusal. But I'm coming to your office to sign, it requires notarized signatures. How about 2:30?" He agreed, and she sent it.

Alone in her office, she recognized the tantalizing love-hate grip this man had on her. *Can I muster the ruthlessness I need?* She half-whispered, "Oh shut up." Then as if rallying herself, "You can do this."

She left her desk, flopped on the sofa and gazed at the expensively furnished office, which she'd decorated herself. In university, for fun, she'd taken interior design as an escape from her heavy workload, *maybe I should've been a designer?* His long, lean physique had graced this sofa and as her thoughts drifted, warmth surfaced. She'd seen him in action, dealing with company presidents, bankers, military brass and high-tech geniuses and he was constantly a step ahead of them, anticipating their needs, answering their questions, rebutting their objections. *Is he a step ahead of me?*

CHAPTER THREE

A half-hour later she was at her condo. After too much peanut butter, she was walking in and out of the closet and admonishing herself. *You make multi-million-dollar decisions but can't pick an outfit for a meeting that you've decided isn't any different than dozens you've had before.* It wasn't true, but she had to keep telling herself that.

She'd dealt with similar awkward situations but not with a man like this, a man who constantly disrupted her sexual sanity. So, she devised a plan to solve the conflict. Because if there was no conflict of interest, there would be no problem, and she could rid herself of the conflict if she eliminated the personal interest – hers and his. And if the personal interest was gone, replaced by normal, unattached sex, then it would be a win-win.

So, in addition to the new company rules, she'd formulated a plan with three, friends-with-benefits rules that could mitigated the conflict between money and sex – her financial responsibility and her sexual pleasure. If she was to succumb to her female needs, so be it. But with rules, there would be a red line that he would have to agree to. No romance. No dates, no flowers, no dinners. Just sex with conditions – limited to lust and its immediate aftermath. And no overnights. She was convinced she could do it and control herself, and him. Because from everything she'd seen, he had great self-discipline.

This was about erotic fantasy, nothing more. Which is why she was fussing over what lingerie to wear? Just in case. Because the only time underwear mattered was when someone else was going to see it. So why the indecision? Red? Black? Now peach? Well, peach was her favorite, so peach it was. She looked in the mirror, turned sideways and heard her question, *I wonder how much he really wants me?* Now for the rest. Upscale suit? Neutral color or power suit? Skirt and blouse? Jewelry? She said to the closet, "Fuck Dyson, make a decision." She pattered into the kitchen for another dollop of peanut butter and then went to her dresser, picked a half slip and made a decision. Since she was up to her peach-covered ass in a multi-million-dollar deal, she better look the part. A power suit.

Apogee's spectacular offices, an architectural sweep of steel, glass and greenery triggered memories from last night – good and bad. She was escorted to his office.

"Victoria." He came around the desk and shook her hand. And let go quickly. *Looks like a million bucks – actually, four-hundred million.* She was stunningly dressed in a taupe designer suit, chocolate colored, high-neck blouse, and expensive heels. He couldn't help thinking how great she'd look no matter what she wore. Even a snowsuit couldn't hide those perfect curves, delightful breasts and oh-so-long-sexy legs. Her eyes showed no recollection of last night. She was a contradiction. On one hand, beautiful and captivating; on the other, independent and uncompromising. A tough, formidable adversary and an erotic wet dream, all rolled into one. His problem was ignoring the erotic and focusing on the adversarial. Because her increased presence was going to magnify his problem and jeopardize his secrets.

He sat in the chair opposite her. "I fly to DC this evening. Have a late dinner there. Meetings tomorrow. Then to Grenada – international security conference." Her blue eyes absorbed but didn't react. "Gone five days. I suggest we cover essentials now, then get you set up down the hall. You can settle in while I'm away." *That'll buy me time.*

She stiffened slightly. "First, let's get your signature on the authorizations appointing me Chair and CFO."

He barely heard what she was saying. After her announcement, he'd decided that he would concede – for now – because he had to have the money. It poked at his pride to have her Chair the board and it would be no picnic having her hanging all over his every move. But even if she made things tougher, he wasn't going to let her – or anything – stop him from closing this acquisition and becoming a billionaire. She must not find out about his problems, at least until after the deal closed.

They signed the papers and transferred the money. He felt more cordial. As she handed back his pen their fingers touched, gingerly but unmistakable. It prompted an honest comment that he regretted the minute it was out of his mouth. "You realize you'll never understand this business just playing with numbers. Gotta be out there, up to your ears in it – whether it's New York, Washington or Grenada." He couldn't believe he said that. *Maybe it didn't register.* But her eyes said it did. They fixed on his. Then a smile, at the corner of her soft, sexy mouth.

"Maybe I should?"

Her tone was measured, but instinct told him her pondering meant probably, and probably meant he could be in trouble. She was biting her bottom lip and looking inquisitively sexy. He cursed himself. Here he was trying to stay away from this woman, instead he'd inadvertently – maybe subconsciously – suggested she join him on the most important trip of his life. *Maybe it could still be averted?* "The problem on the Grenada trip, I won't be able to get you into meetings. Top-secret, military stuff. And the rest of the conference is boring…. Maybe another time."

She saw the scramble. He was backtracking. Although the emotional strain of four or five days with him would test her self-discipline, she'd already accepted that sex might happen. And she had a plan, some new rules. More importantly, it would be an opportunity to better understand the business they were acquiring and find out what he was hiding. After all, she was about to be Chair and CFO. "I think your idea has merit. Jump in with both feet, so to speak."

He absorbed her smile. She looked happy.

She continued. "The Grenada conference would allow me to meet the Pentagon people, and work on the financials while you're in meetings." A ripple of doubt crossed her mind. *Could she function properly if they succumbed to lust on an idyllic Caribbean island. Would her rules work?* She rationalized. *This is about four-hundred-million-dollars, nothing else – and maybe some great sex … what's wrong with that? She would go.* She also heard the little girl from Indiana, *besides, I've never been to Grenada.* "I'll come."

If she's coming, I've got to prepare. "Okay." He stood up.

It started in her core, at the moment he said, 'okay.' Molten heat rising gradually as he rose in front of her. He stood, and everything stood still. Except her fantasy. She couldn't look away, couldn't let go. She pictured every inch of him under his custom-tailored suit, a spectacular custom-tailored body created for unimaginable pleasure. She was close enough to reach out and put a hand on his leg – squeeze his muscular thigh, hard, then ease between his inner thighs and gently lift his bounty. Then stand up, never letting go of his growing erection, and take his mouth, devour his tongue, press her hardened nipples into his chest … and leave the rest to him.

He was surprised by the power of his arousal. He was about to say good-bye but her declaration of, 'I'll come,' shot through him, severing all thought. The blood rush was exhilarating. He motioned toward one of the sofas and said, "Shall I fill you in on the trip?" He pushed a key on his laptop and the blinds closed, shutting out the rest of the office, the rest of the world. She rose like a lioness, her hand brushing him as she turned. He waited to see her walk, needing to let her perfectly designed, undulating ass stir his masculine urges. She reclined in the sofa, in complete control of her body – and his mind. She crossed her legs as if to say, you can look but don't touch … yet. He stared. And repressed the need to force himself deep into the heat beckoning from between her elegant limbs. He had to get a grip. This had to be managed.

She patted the cushion next to her. "Let's talk." She watched him ease down, enraptured by the tantalizing bulge in his Italian slacks. "Have you been to Grenada before?"

"Several times," he said. "Beautiful island. You?"

"No." She placed a hand on his leg, just above the knee. Her peach panties moistened. "You'll have to tell me all about it." She cleared her throat. "But first … we need to have a frank conversation? Not about all the business shit. That's mostly taken care of."

He closed his legs to divert her gaze from his arousal. She uncrossed her legs and pressed immaculate fingernails into his leg. "Yale, we both know what's going on here, between us. It's palpable. And it's not like we haven't been here before. We know the rules." She coughed. She was uneasy about broaching her plan, but the genuine anticipation in his eyes pulled her forward. She just hoped he'd agree. If not, she was in for some serious embarrassment. But she'd calculated that embarrassment was better than the risk of their sexual needs getting out of hand and blowing up the deal. They were seasoned professionals and could walk both sides of the street – have their cake and eat it too. With strict rules.

"Let's make some rules? An agreement between us. Just for us. For now. To get us to the end of this acquisition. And through Grenada. Then we can tear up the agreement, figuratively speaking. Nothing in writing. Just a handshake. Something to handle this sexual insanity between us." Rising heat constricted in her throat.

He responded. "Agree. We can make it work. Full disclosure. Open. Honest." He couldn't deny himself. Or her. "No strings."

"That's rule number one, no personal attachment." She moved closer, her hand moving up his thigh. "Two more rules." Her lips brushed his ear as she whispered.

He heard them. His arousal heightened. He would gladly follow her rules – at least try – to the culmination of every sexual fantasy he'd ever had about her. He put a hand on top of hers just before it touched his rock-hard cock. "I need a minute." He got up, awkwardly, and locked the door.

She never took her eyes off him, or his erection, unfolding like a new born colt inside his pants. She wanted to maintain control just a little longer. As he approached, she said in a throaty whisper, "Rule two … first, my demands."

He stopped, three feet in front of her. "Okay."

She pointed. "Back up against your desk. Plant your gorgeous butt on the edge, and take off your shirt and tie … slowly." Seated on the sofa, she faced him and opened her legs, pulling her skirt up her thighs. As his tie fell to the floor she touched herself. She was only a few degrees away from erupting pleasure. She too must go slow, savor every image from her nights alone with nothing more than unadulterated fantasies and tangled bedsheets. As his shirt slid off, her fingers pushed into her wetness. His magnificent chest and sculpted pecs, with a dabbling of dark hair, moved in rhythm with abs that looked like they'd been carved from stone. Her nails dug into her heat. It pinched. She liked it. He unbuckled his belt. She whispered, "Not yet."

How could he stop? My god, he had no control. She was in control. He jammed both hands in his pockets to restrain them. His imagination and reality slammed together, screaming for her heat and hungering to inhale the sweet aroma of her sex. He couldn't take much more.

She loved the silence. And his stance, hands rammed in his pockets, cock hungry for her. But she wasn't finished with him. She yanked her skirt above her panties and splayed her legs, moving her fingers into her silkiness and pressing against her clitoris, never removing her peach panties. The sound of her wetness drove her to rapid titillation and as her head thrust back she saw him push his pants and boxers to the floor … her fantasy. Hard. Big. Strong. Powerful.

He groaned. "Rule three." But didn't wait for a reply. He sheathed his cock in a condom, took one stride, reached two hands under her ass, locked her legs around him, and buried his unrelenting hardness into her flooding heat.

"Fuck the rules," he shouted.

She engulfed him. Commanded him. Controlled him ... for the moment.

• • •

As she slipped into the limousine, heading for the airport, her legs still moved as if she was floating. The hours after the most incredible sex she'd ever experienced were a wondrous, warm blur. After recovering some energy, they'd stuck to the rules and avoided anything romantic, although he was very attentive and gentle. After dressing, he'd brought her a bottle of water and kissed her, igniting her again. But they restrained, and he said, "I'll leave you alone for now if you go home and pack whatever you need for the flight to Washington. Wheels up at 7:00. And bring a sexy bikini for Grenada." Obviously, he didn't understand women and packing, especially for five days in the tropics. She stopped at Bergdorf's on the way home, picking up some must-haves, at a ridiculous price, even on sale.

She was seated in the lounge at the private terminal contemplating their freshly consummated, erotic addiction, and reminding herself of the need to dig into his secrets. Apparently, after the short flight to Washington, he had a dinner scheduled with some woman. *What the hell's that about?*

He strode in at 6:50, "Sorry I'm late. Traffic." He came over and kissed her. *Wow. That's nice. Chalk it up as sweet, not romantic.* He took her arm and head for the jet.

"Garen will get your bags." He was rushing even though there was no need. It was adrenalin and the anticipation of being alone with her. As they crossed the tarmac, he caught a whiff of her fragrance, not perfume, just the same natural scent he'd indulged in a few hours earlier. As she climbed the stairs onto the plane, he paused to enjoy the blood rush as her most perfect ass, in the most perfect dress, entered his kingdom of luxury.

Private jets were not new to her but this … *OMG*. The interior was the largest she'd ever seen and was custom-designed to somebody's very particular tastes. His. There was the galley and seats for crew, partitioned off from the main cabin, which was decorated in a palette of fawn-colored leather, dark rich wood and stainless-steel trim. In addition to eight plush seats there was a beautiful sofa opposite a slim cabinet with a TV and fresh flowers on it. She hoped the flowers were standard accessories, not a romantic indication. The sofa triggered her sexual fantasies and clouded the simple decision as to where to sit. His hand touched the small of her back.

"Pick a seat, any seat, there's just you and me … and Captain Garen, co-pilot Kate and service by the beautiful Tasha."

Her mind was a whirl in sexual fantasy, imagining him naked on the sofa, his hot ass on the cool leather … or her on the table. She couldn't think. He eased her toward a chair. "Buckle in here until were airborne."

He took a chair, swiveled toward her and touched her knee. "Are you by any chance a white-knuckler?"

"Not at all. Just amazed at your office-in-the-air. Fabulous."

"All the comforts of home away from home. Tables to work on and seats that recline into beds for sleeping. Or …" He winked.

One more wink and I'll take you before take-off. "And the sofa?"

"Opens into a double bed." He winked again.

Geez. Now you've made my new red panties wet.

He said, "Let's get a drink before take-off." He turned, "Tasha."

A pretty woman – very pretty – poked her head out of the galley and smiled.

"I'm having my usual. And Victoria will have …?

She knew his usual, a very dry martini. "Same … be great."

Tasha delivered two martinis, returned to the galley and closed the door dividing the cabins. The whine of the engines revved to a throaty pitch and pushed onto a runway that led, not just to Washington, but to unknown heights of personal pleasure and risk, a risk to the things she'd dedicated her life to – money and independence.

He slowly sucked the third olive off the silver toothpick and savored the best tasting martini he had ever had. It wasn't the martini he was tasting, it was Victoria. Savoring the olive like he intended to savor her as soon as the seat belt sign was off. He saw the excitement in her eyes and felt it in his groin. She knew, he knew. As the jet engines lifted them into the heavens, everything became one world, their world, their sanctuary.

The first ding sounded as the seat-belt sign went off and the second as he activated the 'Do not disturb' light in the crew cabin. "You were wondering about the sofa?"

I was? "Uh … it's exquisite."

"Italian, vegetable tanned, grain leather. Soft as a baby's bum." He held his handsome hands up and smiled. "Hand-picked."

She whispered. "You just had to say that didn't you?"

He gave her a puzzled smile.

"Bum … had to say it, right?" She was playing. "You're the bum … for being so damn sexy."

"Sexy? Me? Look who's talking."

"You're not only a brilliant investor, you're a wine connoisseur, a leather connoisseur … and a sex connoisseur." She captured his eyes. "Tell me, are you a table connoisseur?" She looked at the table.

"Mahogany. Very strong. Has a pull-out leaf. Seats four." His eyes pulled her in. "Hand-made." He held his hands up again. "But not by these hands."

She stood in front of him and took his hands. "These hands have a more important purpose." She placed them on her hips, ran her hands through his hair and pulled his head against her tummy. "And they better be quick … before the seat-belt sign goes on again."

Her scent overwhelmed his nostrils, surging to every part of his body. In one upward rush, he stood, lifting her dress and capturing her buttocks in powerful hands. His body was harsh in its hunger, pressing against her demanding heat. She opened to him, mouth, arms, legs. He drank her in … and then released her.

Nooo. A gasp of heat slipped from her lips.

Holding her waist, he swung her around, pulled her buttocks into his groin, nestled his head into the crook of her neck. "Put your beautiful hands on that hand-crafted mahogany table and – "

Without a word, she bent over, arching her hips, opening up to him. He yanked her panties down and his pants and briefs fell to the floor. The condom went on and his hardness thrust between her legs, driving into her heat. Hard. Harsh. Ravenous. Buried in her glory, he touched her clitoris and with the other hand held her hips in a vice-like grip, relentlessly pounding his throbbing cock into her releasing wet. Her heat was overwhelming, and she screamed as she came. He stretched his limits for a moment, then shuddered and exploded in gratification. He quivered inside her, groaning as her vibrating muscles contracted and came again.

"Did I mention the table was Italian."

"Is this cabin sound proof?"

"No idea. Never asked."

She said. "Couch looks very soft. She rolled onto the couch with a long, soft sigh. "You should come with a warning label … Beware orgasms – "

"Beware nothing, enjoy everything." He went to the washroom, disposed of the condom, washed up, slipped his pants on and eased onto the couch next to her. He felt different. She was different. It was different. And he wasn't sure what to do with 'different.' Involuntarily, he put his hand on her leg, above her still bare knee. "This is all because of your second rule. That your demands must come first, that you get to decide when, where – ”

“Why is it my fault?” She didn't move his hand. Couldn't. *It's just for a moment.* “This is your jet. You made the sexual innuendo about your handcrafted table being strong and – ”

“Just being the most unbelievably sexy woman is in itself a demand. A demand I can't ignore, I have to – ”

“Ah ha! See, it's your fault. You can't ignore what you should ignore, no self-discipline. It's not my demand, it's you. You have no control.” She was playful. “That's why I have to be in control. That's what rule number two is about.” She stood up. “You sit here and get yourself under control while I freshen up. Can't arrive in Washington looking like this … hell, Tasha might suspect we'd had sex back here.” Her smile was teasing and happy.

When she returned he was on his phone, so she took the plush chair opposite him. A little distance would help avoid any recurring fantasies before they landed. With him just a few feet away, close enough to catch a whiff of his delicious aroma, she had to be strong. As she looked across the evening sky, she heard an inner voice ask, *what are you doing here Victoria Leigh Dyson? This is a long way from West Lafayette, Indiana.* Although she'd been playing in the big leagues for several years, right now things seemed almost too good, too much.

She'd received her undergraduate degree from Purdue University in just three years and was one of the youngest graduates from Wharton's MBA program, majoring in economics and finance, summa cum laude. She did a stint at Deloitte in forensic investigations, then joined the Blackstone Group, and then Kennor Capital. She'd done well and made her Daddy proud, although he'd died of Lou Gehrig's disease three months after she joined Kennor. His death had been hard for her because she was his protégé. He'd been a professor of economics at Purdue and her personal mentor. She had twin brothers, Gene and Geoff, who were ten years older. On their eighteenth birthday Gene was killed in a car accident.

Devastating. Changed everybody's lives, forever. Her mother, the weak link in the family, became an emotional cripple. Geoff was never the same. Her dad just got stronger. He channeled much of his attention to his "little Flamingo." Long before the feminism movement, her father had believed women were better suited to leadership than men and he'd often said to her, 'Don't let anyone tell you that you can't be kind, caring, sensitive and still be tough, aggressive and decisive. It's a wonderful combination that many women come by naturally, while men can't get these opposing traits together. They opt for just tough and aggressive.' Her accomplishments have all been with the quiet voice of her father as a companion, and today she wished he could be with her. He would have loved this jet. But he would say, *first the necessary, then the useful, then the pleasant.*

CHAPTER FOUR

In the limo, Yale talked about the importance of getting a commitment from the Pentagon. "The head guy will be in Grenada. It's essential that I confirm his commitment so that – "

"Let me ask you," she interrupted. "I was going through the financials and noticed you still haven't completed your medical disclosure forms." *I think he flinched.*

"Victoria, you know I'm not good at details." He shrugged. "I'll get them done."

His zest-for-life smile washed her thoughts away. *Later …*

He had dinner arranged with his ex-lawyer Zofia, but stupidly, on the plane, in a post-intercourse rush of lust, he'd suggested that he and Victoria meet for a drink in the lounge, first. He knew it was his lack of discipline – and her allure.

As soon as he was in his hotel room, he called Apogee's controller, Bernie Solomon. He got voice mail. "Bernie, she's scrutinizing everything. She's bound to ask more questions. Which I'll deal with. But I want the files we spoke about kept under wraps until after I close the deal. Protect them on the server. I'll call tomorrow."

He found the lounge, but not her. As she arrived, he'd ordered a second scotch, "Glenfiddich please." *How could one woman look so good in so many outfits.* She'd changed into a dark red dress that hugged her slim hips exactly as the designer envisioned it. His fascination rushed to his groin, his mind wandered.

She nodded at the waiter. "Same, on the rocks, water on the side."

"I've got something for you," he said.

I know … already had some.

"Call it homework." He put a flash stick on the table. "Files on our potential customers, including the Pentagon. You'll see detailed profiles on the two people we'll be meeting. Be a good if you get up to speed."

She didn't reach for it. "Since I'm new on the job, I don't think they'll expect me to be up to speed. I'm sure you can handle that. But I'll review it. Going to stick to the financials for now." She picked up the stick.

She eased the scotch over her lips. He was acting more like her Jekyll and Hyde again. Was he trying to create obstacles? He looked relaxed, leaning back in the chair, legs crossed, twiddling a swizzle stick between his fingers – *such nimble fingers*. She had to quell her inner stirrings. "By the way, who is the woman you're having dinner with? Company business? Or should I mind my own business?"

"No, no." He waved his hand. "Indirectly, it's business. My ex-lawyer Zofia Gorka. You probably saw her name on some old documents. She handled some of the original legal work for Xcryption. She's based in Washington. Well connected. I want to see if she has any new insight into the Pentagon. Before we get to Grenada."

Picking up her phone she asked, "I've got the conference agenda here. Should we set a working schedule for Grenada? To finalize financials. Can't close the deal until they're final."

"Sure." He loved to watch her … lips forming words, crossing her legs, shifting her bum in the chair. He suspected it was the subconscious reason for suggesting the drink, just to be with her a little longer. She had a calm intensity about her, an undiscovered depth. It enticed and disrupted him. He also suspected he did it because he wasn't looking forward to dinner with Zofia – a history he did not want to revisit.

She went over the conference agenda and scheduled times. "What about after dinner on Friday evening?"

"Not a chance," he said. "That's the formal dinner – speeches, awards and dancing. Grenada's annual carnival starts that day. Huge event; practically takes over the island. You'll enjoy it."

"Okay." She pressed send. "Just sent you our schedule." She sipped the scotch, set it down and stood up. "See ya' in the morning?"

"Yep" *My god she's gorgeous.* "First meeting 8:30. Then eleven. Wheels up at two." "Night."

"Night…."

As she walked away his eyes lingered, as usual. What wasn't usual was the feeling that crossed the lounge with her, disappointment that she was leaving, and an uncontrollable desire that was not healthy for his own good, or the good of the deal.

She felt his eyes – more than she should.

Later in the darkness of her room, waiting for sleep, she could still feel them. She wondered how admiring they were? How wanting? Lustful? As sexual fantasy gave way to sleep, she reminded herself that her new rules would be put to the test on the flight tomorrow.

• • •

At the rude sound of the alarm, Victoria opened one eye. The digital clock stared back: 6:00 am. Her lingering was cut-short with the realization that she had to call her office before breakfast. She showered, gave her hair a brisk towel-dry and put on her favorite T-shirt from her alma mater, Purdue. It was a reminder of a distant past. And a distant memory that she sometimes rekindled while lying in bed, alone – an earlier love that sometimes helped her feel better.

It was a memory that had vanished when she met Yale. But now, with her feelings adrift in the void between no-strings sex and unimagined emotions, she needed to cling to this real-life fantasy, which had always helped when caught in her all-work-no-play life. There'd never been a shortage of men, especially in the rarified air of high finance and rich playboys. But none were serious. Her relationships were on her terms, a take-it-or-leave-it basis, just short-term pleasure along her road to ambition. Never getting in the way of where she wanted to go. She wanted the glamor, yes. Excitement, yes. Sexual pleasure, for sure. Companionship, sometimes. Love, never. But way-back-when, when she was at Purdue, there was a man. A man she'd not forgotten. She'd fallen in love – at least that's what it felt like then.

He was a pilot, Kelly Kranston. His middle name was Keith. His father, Bud Kelly, dubbed him KKK. The ol'man, being from Alabama, thought it was clever, but his son considered it a bad joke. He'd rebelled against his repressive father and left home when he was sixteen and earned his pilot's license before he was twenty-two. He went by Kelly K. or KK. They met in the summer between her junior and senior year when she was working at a resort in Maine. She was nineteen, he was twenty-nine. She met him on a short-hop flight from Boston to Portland. He spotted her when he strolled through the cabin and then helped with her bags, bought her a coffee and found out where she was working. He was a hunk. Tall, rugged with adventurous green eyes that were always chasing something – excitement, hope, risk. She had a thing for adventure, and always liked on-the-edge-of-the-seat movies and fantasized about tough, take-no-shit, anti-heroes, the 'bad boys' – like Michael Douglas in *Wall Street*, James Gandolfini in *The Sopranos*, Damian Lewis in *Billions*, And she had a 'thing' for uniforms. Kelly's pilot uniform fit his athletic body like a glove, like she imagined his hands fitting every inch of her body.

The next week he visited her at the resort. It felt like love at first sight, at least love as a nineteen-year-old understood it. Infatuation, lust and excitement all rolled into one. On her day off, he whisked her away for a ride in a single-engine, float plane. She didn't like little planes but steeled herself for the adventure, too taken by his carefree spirit to say anything. And part of her ate it up. It was like being a James Bond woman. She felt bold, wild and sexy. After about thirty minutes in the air – flying way too close to the tree tops as far as she was concerned – he landed the plane on a lake that looked too small. But he did it as if this wasn't the first time he'd landed there. He eased the plane up to the rickety dock of an abandon hunting lodge and as she stepped out of the plane it was as if she was stepping into a movie. Anticipation surged and their walk in the woods was a walk on the wild side. Her nineteen-year old libido was as high as the cloudless sky and her sexual appetite soared beyond the towering pines. He talked about some of his adventures and extreme sports, from bungie jumping in the Grand Canyon to the Running of the Bulls in Spain. He was reliving each story and used every four-letter word she'd ever heard. When he said them, they weren't crude, they were exciting. He said the word 'fuck' with such emotion and regularity that she was fantasizing about him long before he kissed her. He'd just finished telling her about a-near-death accident he'd had in the Rocky Mountains, when a horse unexpectedly reared over the prone body of a woman lying stuck in the snow. 'It was fuckin' scary. There was nothin' I could do. His two, fucking hoofs came down on each side of her head. Missed by inches … fuck! I'll never forget the look on her face. As I picked her up, she burst into tears. I'm tellin' ya' … was fuckin' scary…. But fuckin' exciting.' He stopped in the trail. Cupped her face in his muscular hands and kissed her. Hard. Deep. Then he picked her up and headed for the lodge. Her voice whispered as she released her femininity. "Here … here … under the trees."

The summer sky wrapped her in its heat, the pine needles scratched her nakedness and the sound of the wind murmured 'this is love.' It mirrored the sexual fantasy of a nineteen-year-old. The ground was rough, KK was rough, and he growled out dirty commands. He was lost in his own fantasy, maybe leaping off a cliff creating his own orgasmic memory. She remembered it, all of it, every bite, scratch, slap, thrust and inch of pleasure. And until Yale, she would, from time to time, replay her first with KK.

It was a wild summer, a thrill-seeking pursuit of sexual fantasy and make-believe love. Kelly visited often. Sometimes they only had an hour between flights. They had sex in the airport, the car, the woods, a parked plane, a café washroom and on a huge boulder at the edge of the Atlantic Ocean. It was intense and crazy when he was there. Then he was gone, and she was free until he returned. She loved it. It was her indoctrination into what became her dual need to pursue sexual passion while holding onto female independence. He gave her that, and more. Then he died. Less than a year later, he crashed a twin-engine Cessna into a hillside during a violent storm, somewhere in Pennsylvania. The agony and loss was embedded in her and too often rolled out from the night darkness and laid naked with her when she tried to sleep. The loss of Kelly probably exacerbated her attachment disorder, which comes from her mom's lack of care during her childhood. Detachment has always been normal for her. But Yale was magnifying the conflict between her growing sexual fantasies and her fear of attachment.

After room service delivered green tea, she sent a bunch of e-mails and called Andrea Garcia, head of administration at Kennor Capital. "Morning Andrea."

"Morning."

"On my way to Grenada."

"Grenada?"

She filled Andrea in – only the business, not the personal – and then added some levity. "Of course, I had to buy a couple of outfits suitable for the tropics. Found a great sale at Bergdorf's yesterday. Most fun I've had in months. But a sale at Bergdorf's still isn't what ya'd call a sale ... but what the hell." She chuckled. "You should see the beaded dress I picked up. You'd love it. Beads sound garish, but this is a slipdress, Michael Kors Collection. Exquisite. Cocoa brown with opalescent beads on the trim, on the straps and up both sides of a six-inch slit on the left thigh. Perfect for evenings. Of course, I had to buy a jacket to go with it. And I got a lovely off-white, linen suit. Don't ask how much. And a swimsuit – black. All for less than five thousand. Some sale!" She laughed with Andrea. It felt good to be connected back to where things were more certain. Since her first day at Kennor, Andrea had been her anchor. "Enough about my fashion spree. I need to know more about Xcryption's past. About the previous owner, how he acquired the company, etcetera, etcetera." She paused to let Andrea catch up. "You'll need a private investigator. Get Ryan Todd. I'll take whatever you come up with by end of day tomorrow. The rest on an as-you-get-it basis…. Gotta go."

The morning in Washington went well and watching him in action was fascinating, in more ways than one. It inflamed her conflicts. He was all gentleman, all professional and made her feel his equal throughout the meetings. But despite his outward confidence, he was quieter than usual, and she sensed something was bothering him. When she inquired, she got a curt denial.

Yale was exhilarated having Victoria at his side and all went well, except he couldn't stop thinking about the news Zofia had dropped on him last night. A reliable source said that 'some people' were inquiring about the Xcryption acquisition and planning a counter offer. Worse, the interested parties were questionable – as in criminal. Victoria must not find out.

CHAPTER FIVE

By two-fifteen they were at thirty thousand feet, ensconced in luxury and sipping his favorite Napa Valley Chardonnay. *My off-white linen suit matches this interior perfectly.* When not thinking about the real reason for being with him, she was comfortable, and he was his good-natured self. He was on and off the phone, so she was reading Forbes.

After a call he said, "Thought you'd be relaxing and reading Vogue?"

"Goes to show, can't tell a woman by the cover."

"Doesn't all work and no play make Victoria a dull girl?"

The cliché reverberated in her head, pulling her back to when her same question triggered their first, close encounter. She saw the memory in his eyes. "Dull, as in last night on that table?"

His head shook. "Right. Your new rules changed all that. I mean before – "

"What do you really mean?" She was pushing but couldn't stop. "What does this sex palace in the sky really mean to you?

"You mean, to us?"

"No. To you."

He paused. "It's wonderful … a great perk. But perks aren't everything." He touched her leg, just above the knee and squeezed. "Last night, you were everything."

Every nerve-ending responded. She couldn't.

"You realize we skipped right past rule number two, to rule three – my demands. With complete disregard for your demands, your control." His eyes held her. "You were the complete opposite of dull … mesmerizing. I needed to devour you. And took advantage of you. Needed to."

She found a whisper. "I needed you. Had no control. Didn't want it."

As he stood up her sexual energy rose with him, racing to every extremity of her body. She watched, floating on air, as he unfolded the couch into a bed. She was only aware of his gentleness, his spreading a white linen sheet over the leather, fluffing pillows, removing her clothes and laying her down in only her underwear. He stretched out next to her, naked, and she folded into his embrace, control giving way to possession, memory succumbing to the moment.

At some point, somewhere in the distance, she heard the hum of the engines, just beyond her cocoon of pleasure. She was barely aware of him getting up and going to the washroom as she fought against returning to reality – she preferred the alternative. Then he was there, standing over her.

"Welcome back Beautiful."

She managed a smile. He handed her a robe and kissed her.

Ten minutes later she was watching him on the phone. Then he turned his attention to her, trying to act nonchalant, as if everything was normal. Even though everything was not. The fantasies had been vivid and graphic but the real thing, the real him, was … beyond description. In fact, she couldn't remember what had just happened, no specific memory of what he did, what she did, when she climaxed, when he did … nothing. It was as if she'd traveled to another world and returned with no conscious memory, just blissful elation … *an alien abduction without the spaceship – just his jet?* It was perhaps beyond her imagination. Whatever it was, she loved it. And maybe when she returned to her senses, she'd remember. For now, the bliss was more than enough.

His smile was extra warm. "So much for 'dull.' Your name and dull should never, ever, be used in the same sentence. You're beyond words."

"You don't need words. Your actions speak louder."

"I was thinking." He had a boyish twinkle in his eyes. "You obviously drive yourself too hard so maybe it's time for a break, some R&R? No better place than an idyllic Caribbean island."

She raised an eyebrow.

"You should take some time and visit the small island of Carriacou … a paradise. Great ferry boat ride, about ninety minutes north of Grenada."

Her yearning was just beneath the surface. A *picturesque island, boat rides, him.* He was right; she could use some R&R. What if they didn't have the conflict between business and pleasure? What if the pleasure was allowed to flourish, go wherever it wanted? Imagine the next few days. She'd love to be at his side, watch him, listen to him, hold him. His potent physique. She imagined him on the beach in a bathing suit. A flush coursed through her skin and her nipples responded. She squeezed her thighs to quell the impulse. She had to get back to business. *Damn conflict.* "I'm sure you could use some R&R too. But we're short on time. Nice thought. But ..." She shrugged and tried to regain some control. *Somebody had to.* "Maybe I'll come back someday, no business, just pleasure. Sounds like you've been here before?"

"Several times. Sailed the Grenadines and most of the Caribbean."

"Doesn't sound like business?"

"Sometimes tacked on a week of sailing."

"Big boat?"

"Bareboat. Sailed all my life."

"With crew."

"Just need one person. Can do it myself but ... Hey, how'd you like to do a day-sail? While we're here. You and me?" He was beaming. That wild spirit again. "Yes, yes. What do you say?"

For that smile, there was only one answer. *Fuck the conflict of interest.* "Okay. But where do you get a boat on short notice?"

"Leave that to me. We'll juggle the schedule. Do it Saturday." He made a call. "Heather, can you get hold of Ambrose. Tell him to have *Deckadence* in St. George's a day earlier. By Friday night. Tell him to confirm." He turned to her. "We're good to go."

She suppressed her excitement. *My god, alone with him on a sailboat ... must get back to business.* "How did the meeting go last night with ... 'er, what's her name?" She hadn't forgotten the name, just had a hard time saying it. Which was stupid because it, she, should mean nothing to her. Just his ex-lawyer. And probably an ex-lover. *That's it. Jealousy. Stupid. Grow up girl.*

"Zofia," he said half-heartedly. "Okay. Just wanted to see if she had any news."

"And."

"Nothing much."

He was uncomfortable. But if it had any effect on the acquisition, she should know about it. This is where conflict raised its ugly head. She had to press him, even though the only pressing she wanted to do was beautiful, not ugly. "Look, I get that she played a role in the past and might be helpful now, but my concern is whether she might do something to jeopardize the deal." She wasn't getting eye contact. "It's my responsibility, along with you, to make this deal work, no matter what. And if Zofia has to be involved, so be it."

His voice was calm but his face shadowed. "It's complicated. "

"Try me."

"As you know, she's a lawyer and a partner in Xcryption. What you don't know – few people do – she's JK's daughter and – "

"What?"

"It's actually to our advantage. She's on our side."

"How's that?" *Your side maybe. I'm not so sure about my side.* "And by the way, what ever happened to full disclosure?"

"It's in the agreement." He added, "the fine print."

This is the part she hated. Him turning from Dr. Jekyll to Mr. Hyde. He went on to explain Zofia's role in the past and how he now needed her to sign over her shares in order to stop JK from reneging on the deal. By the time he was finished, she been emotionally whipsawed between caring and anger. There was too much he hadn't told her before and yet, she admire his brilliance and that he had a plan to save the deal. Their deal. What she didn't like was that Zofia had become crucial to the deal.

Why was he touchy about Zofia? The business connection wasn't new, but the fact that he now had to work with her to close the deal bugged her. Shouldn't. But it did. *Another fucking conflict.* She attempted her best hard-ass stare. "Look, do what you have to do with her but if she gets in the way, I'll catch the next flight back to the US and pull the funds." She'd drawn a line. Would he step over? She waited. The tension in his jaw subsided.

"There's no need to play hardball with your bags of money. You're making too much of this. She's not a problem, she can help us." It was part plea, part demand. "And let's not air this dirty laundry in front of the Pentagon people. You hold the purse strings, but that purse is dependent on their multi-billion-dollar contract. And I'm the only one who can get it signed by next week." He touched her arm and then glared into the emptiness outside.

She absorbed him. His energy. His contradictions. His predicament. His secrets. She stirred. She couldn't separate the good and bad – didn't want to – and couldn't divide him into separate pieces, like a cold business project and a hot personal adventure. He was a whole package, brilliant and dark, all in one. Her package. Her dilemma. Her conflict – in the world of big money.

Since graduating from Wharton, she'd had a meteoritic rise and learned from mentors on how to focus on the money and compartmentalize the personal. And even though she was young for her level of achievement, she'd proven she could be financially ruthless. Until now.

Here she was, the whiz kid from West Lafayette, exactly where she wanted to be, in the world of high finance, flying on a private jet to an exotic place and in charge of a multi-million-dollar deal. And yet, she was straining to separate business from personal, money from love – or whatever it was. She studied his anguish, framed by the circular window and the vast unknown just beyond, and wondered if she would ever really know him. In this moment, on this jet, she simply wanted to hold him. No business. No rules. No arguing. Just hold him. Then kiss him, first lightly on his cheek, then softly on the lips, then deep in his mouth, then down his neck, chest, thighs and then swallow up his troubles, pain, secrets and passion in a wave of unadulterated hunger.

He turned. "Have to make a call." And before he was finished, the pilot announced the landing.

As they disembarked into the tropical heat, he took her arm, guiding her down the stairs and into an uncertain future.

When she entered her room overlooking the spectacular sweep of Grand Anse Beach she soaked up the splendor. Then called room service. After much negotiation – the woman on the phone must have thought she was weird – she was able to order two servings of toast and ten small packets of peanut butter. The peanut butter didn't help and facing four days of vacillating between protecting four-hundred million dollars and controlling her unquenchable desire for him, she opted for a cold shower. *Am I doing this for the love of money, or the love of what money gets me, or something I don't understand … love?*

That evening she ate alone in her room. He had invited her to the opening conference dinner but she'd said, 'Thanks, but no thanks.' She was not up for another round in the battle between her sexual needs and her waning discipline. And being beside him but not able to touch him would exhaust her. She didn't need to be with a bunch of strangers in a noisy sound chamber of small talk. She preferred the company of herself and her good friend peanut butter. And a chance to gather her thoughts. *What would her father say?*

Charley Dyson had a pithy observation for almost every situation and she smiled as one of his favorites resonated. When faced with a problem he always said, 'Bring it on.' And that's what she kept telling herself in her topsy-turvy experience. The multi-million-dollar deal came first and had to be anchored in a non-emotional relationship, the personal side be damned. And she'd made some rules to keep the emotion out of it, 'friends with benefits.' Except the benefits were overpowering, way beyond her imagination. She was the problem. Sure, she was a tough, independent business woman and as strong and capable as any guy standing on the glass ceiling, but she had a fear of failure that too often raised its yappy voice, especially when she needed to admit a mistake or reveal a fault. It stemmed from not wanting to disappoint her father. She'd never told him about her torrid love affair with Kelly, even though she was a deliriously happy, coming-of-age woman. Because she knew he would have questioned her judgement. And she never shared Kelly's death with him. Then there was the other secret she never shared with her father or mother. At age twenty-four, she'd gotten pregnant and they would have been horrified. Her father was great, but myopic about certain things, all related to his overly strict, Christian upbringing. And she never had to tell them because of an early-term miscarriage. It was her secret and to this day she hung onto it, and its consequences.

CHAPTER SIX

A wet dawn crept over Grand Anse Bay as Yale paced behind closed doors. He would have preferred opening the patio sliders to the sound of the sea, but he'd been on the phone since five and it was critical he wasn't overheard. "Are you certain? This isn't fake news?" His face was as gray as the rain-soaked dawn. The longer he listened the more his muscular shoulders drooped and the slower his pace. He slumped into a chair. "Thanks Bernie ... get back to ya." With elbows on knees, he dropped his head in his hands. He greeted the morning with an audible curse.

Bernie Solomon had confirmed that some hack blogger was inquiring about a rumored, third party buyer. It was a serious threat. And if it got too far it could expose the secret he must keep from Kennor Capital, Victoria and the Pentagon. They must not know that J.K. was, in addition to a real estate tycoon, an arms dealer. The danger now was that if a second-rate blogger got digging into this, it could expose everything. He had to move fast.

JK was a wealthy real estate developer, surrounded by dubious people and often involved in questionable deals, but the encryption software used by Xcryption was patented and very valuable, which is why Yale wanted the deal, despite the risks. The success of Xcryption could be his holy grail, it had the potential to be a multi-billion-dollar company. He knew it. Kennor knew it. But now, just days from finalizing the deal, it could fall apart. It was contingent on the Pentagon signing a contract with Xcryption before JK backed out of the deal.

J.K. Kondraki had emigrated from Poland after WWII and

was a bricklayer who had amassed a fortune, first in the building trades, then in real estate. Yale had never looked into the source of his wealth, but realized JK was far wealthier than his real estate holdings were worth. The sale of Xcryption wasn't much more than pocket change to JK, but if the Pentagon or Kennor or Victoria got a whiff of JK's other business, the deal could collapse.

JK had placed thirty-three percent of Xcryption ownership in Zofia's name, probably to park them somewhere safe from his wife. Victoria and Kennor were aware of Zofia's ownership but they didn't know that JK, a domineering father controlled the family and her holdings. He was the type of man who would throw his own daughter under the bus to get what he wanted. After JK had agreed to sell to Apogee, one of his clients, a small nation, wanted the software and was offering $800 million and he was determined to get out of his deal with Apogee. But he had two problems. One, he had to wait until the Pentagon signed. And two, he had to have his daughter's consent because she was a one-third partner.

Yale's plan was to get the Pentagon on board and hold JK off until he could get Zofia to sell her shares to Apogee. And make sure she didn't divulge, out of spite or unintentionally, his personal secret. Zofia hated her father's nefarious dealings but she was too frightened to go against him.

So far, he'd failed to convince her to go against him because she was not about to risk losing her multi-billion-dollar inheritance for the mere pittance Apogee and Kennor would pay for her 33% – about $166 million. Somehow, he had to find a way to open her heart until the deal was done. But if her heart became exposed, she could be an even bigger problem. Their relationship, although it appeared to have ended amicably, had badly damaged her fake self-esteem and she was a woman scorned. With Victoria's presence – and jealousy being Zofia's middle name – it was an unpredictable storm he must avoid. He was in bed, figuratively speaking, with two diametrically different women and he had to make sure

Victoria didn't get entangled.

• • •

Victoria's patio door was open to the sound of the wind, rain and waves. Here she was in a king size bed, alone, wondering what was next in her life. She peeked at the clock – 5:45 – and yanked the sheet over her head. She had forty-five minutes before breakfast in his suite. She felt his presence and her imagination wandered … him, here, under the cool sheets. Like a pilot light, her heat ignited and she stretched out, embracing the fantasy that would soon be fulfilled – at least the sexual part.

Just as she was about to leave the room, Andrea called. "Ryan Todd dug up some dirt on this guy Kondracki. Not pretty. But not confirmed either."

"Give me the abridged version. I'm late."

Andrea explained that Kondracki had a lot of connections with third world characters and might be into gun running, and worse. "Good work. This might be what Walters is hiding – *last names sound more professional.* "Let me know if and when he confirms. Gotta run."

The minute he opened the door she knew something was wrong. He looked like shit. No smile. Dark eyes. "Morning," and he went to the kitchenette for coffee.

"Good morning to you too," she said, putting her bag on a chair. He didn't offer a coffee.

"Room service on the way," he grumped.

She scanned what was called The President's Suite, an extravagant backdrop for its disconsolate guest. As he brooded, she took a stroll. An expansive, open living room decorated in a wonderful blend of tropical colors with half-a-dozen overstuffed chairs and a large sectional sofa looking over a sweeping balcony and the ocean. There were more places to sit than any one person could sit on – *or have sex on* – in a week. In the other direction was a long, glass table, with ten chairs covered in a fabric that was a potpourri of island fruits – mango, pineapple, papaya. And embedded in the wall behind the table was a spectacular, salt-water aquarium, maybe fifteen feet long, filled with tropical fish. Looking closely, she saw a little octopus slinking over the coral, changing colors like a chameleon. *Pretty. But ugly. Yucky.* The balcony was filled with white wicker furniture and off the master bedroom was a private patio with a retractable awning and a hot tub tucked into a cozy corner, protected from the wind, and curious eyes. *Fantasy corner.* And the master bedroom. *Wow!* The fireplace seemed out of place in the tropics – maybe they had a few cool nights – but it wasn't the center piece. That was reserved for a raised, four-poster, king-size bed dressed in all-white linens and a muted peach duvet. *Will match my underwear.* She touched a pillow case. Expensive Egyptian cotton. The view from the bed was breathtaking. *OMG, the perfect place for fulfilling erotic fantasies.*

She returned to the living room hoping he'd shed some of his darkness. "Yale … tell me – "

"Let's get to the financials you want to discuss."

She hesitated. "I want to discuss you. You look like shit."

He attempted a grin over a sip of coffee. "Can't say the same about you, you look great."

"I'm serious. Looking ahead, I see we – "

"So you're psychic now … seeing ahead – "

"We can do without the sarcasm. And I do mean 'we,' as in you, me and Ms. Apogee. Our future hangs on this trip." She paused. He was staring out the window, mug in hand. His powerful profile, silhouetted against the morning light, filled her with an involuntary ripple of craving. "Before we get to finances … and before your meetings, you have to be at your best. And you sure as hell ain't lookin' your best right now. If you – "

He didn't turn. "JK is a problem."

The doorbell rang. "How?" She went to the door without taking her eyes off him and quickly signed the room service bill.

His gaze was blank. She couldn't read him.

He said. "What I'm about to tell you could be the end of our deal … of us. But I need you … your help … so…." His eyes dropped.

Her emotions crashed and spiked, all in one sentence. From the 'end of the deal … of us' to 'I need you….' *Did he really mean 'end of us?' Did he really mean, 'I need you?'*

"Got a call from Bernie. There's a rumor that JK is an arms dealer and – "

"What?"

"It's a rumor. Some blogger fishing. It's not – "

"Rumor or not, either way, we're talking the Pentagon, the potential for – "

"I get it. I get it … the consequences?"

His anger was rising. She was drawn to his fire, it made her feel stronger.

"Could be disastrous." He paused. "But it isn't *yet*." He slumped into a chair at the end of the table.

She squatted in front of him, cupping her hands around his and the cold coffee mug. "I've got someone looking into his background and – "

"You what?"

"Confirms your news. Kondracki is a bigger problem than we thought."

"Who's looking into him?"

"Me. Kennor Capital. Our PI."

"Fuck. Why didn't you tell me? If you've got secrets – "

"I was going to."

"If we're not honest, JK will sabotage this deal, he'll – "

"I just found out. Andrea called as I was leaving my room."

"This man has probably killed people – had them killed – for a lot less than what we're taking about."

She squeezed his hands. "The question is, what do we do?"

"If I'm to trust you, we have to – "

"Trust? That cuts both ways. I'll tell you who I don't trust. If – "

"Me. I get it. You don't trust me. But this isn't about me, it's about money. A shit load of money. It's not about me, you … us. There is no us. Just money. And – "

No us? She stood up. "What I was going to say was … I don't trust anybody *but* you in dealing with him. You know him. You brought him to this deal. Only you can clean it up." She moved to the other side of the table. She was still stuck on the '*no us.*' It was like an arrow shot through her lingering hope, and it wasn't cupid's arrow.

He stood. "Like I said, it ain't over 'til it's over."

She saw energy return to his eyes.

"I'll clean it up." He put the coffee cup down and came toward her. "But I can't do it alone. I need you …"

Which is it? Need you? No us?

"… your patience, understanding … your trust. That I will do the right thing for us and close the biggest fuckin' deal of our life. You and me – together – we can pull this off."

His eyes were honest. And filled with … *hope, need?*

He took her hands. "If we put our heads together, pool our resources, work together, we can take this bastard down."

Determination replaced doubt, conviction overtook fear, and something changed. Something imperceptible crossed the divide between them, connecting a deep, common passion. He needed her. She needed him. Yes, the need for money, the love of money. But other needs strained to be released from behind the wall of money.

He related what Bernie and Zofia had said and told her what he knew about Kondracki, which included arms-trading. He talked in a matter-of-fact tone but was animated and determined. "This won't stop me. I'll do whatever it takes."

"*We'll* do whatever it takes."

His phone rang. "Bernie … Thanks." He hung up and stood up. "We need to move. Tell you more as we go." He pointed to the untouched breakfast. "Ya' like cold eggs?"

"Not hungry."

He took her arm and headed for the door. "Let's get your security clearance."

His grip was firm, and she followed his pull, including the pull at her heart.

She loved being with him as he moved through the yakking, yammering coffee guzzlers. He was in his element. Intent. In charge. He introduced her to scientists and bigwigs and the people from the Pentagon. Each time, with a deft touch of her arm, he eased her forward, front and center. She loved his touch.

"Justine, this is Victoria Dyson. Victoria … Justine Cameron, head of procurement at the Pentagon." He turned to the gentleman. "And Major Grant Adams, who heads the department." Everyone shook hands. "Victoria is Chief Financial Officer and Chair of Xcryption … she's in charge of all things connected to money." He set a lunch meeting with them for the next day to review the contract and scheduled the signing for next week.

She began to feel part of the team, like a partnership is supposed to be – in sync, in tune, in lock-step. Together. The morning sessions were boring, scientists and techies rambling on about encryption and coding so at lunch she returned to her room to continue digging into the finances and work on the Kondracki problem. If it didn't get resolved, she'd have to tell Carl Kennor. An hour later Yale knocked on her door and she greeted him dressed in her gray Purdue T-shirt and cotton athletic shorts.

After the rain, it was sticky-hot and he couldn't wait to get into the air conditioning, but he stood under the latticed overhang for a moment, staring at her in the doorway. Whatever words he'd planned to say were stuck somewhere between his eyes and his heart. He was frozen in the heat – if someone can be frozen in heat when gaping at the hottest, most captivating, sexiest woman ever to graduate from Purdue University. She looked like a cheerleader, and if her T-shirt had been wet, it would have been unlawful. And if her shorts clung to her hips any more precariously she would have been arrested. Not knowing what he was thinking he said, "I was thinking – "

"You look like a tropical sweat ball. Come into the air conditioning."

He waited until she turned and walked into the room. *Those shorts, on those hips, covering that perfect ass …*

She looked back. "You coming?"

He held back his instinctive dirty thought and tossed his briefcase on a chair and watched her every motion as she grabbed two bottles of water from the refrigerator. *Nothing is going to cool me down.* "Meetings were brutal. Endless questions about codes and algorithms."

Sitting at the table, she talked about the schedule and a time to meet that evening. They agreed on nine. Then she switched to Kondracki. "How much control does he have over his daughter and do you think – "

He'd had a moment to turn down his inner temperature. "Victoria. I've been thinking … this really doesn't concern you. It's not finances, it's – "

"Excuse me? I have a hundred million reasons – soon to be two hundred – and then four-hundred million reasons to be concerned. This could screw everything up." She hesitated. "Remember, we're in this together."

"Okay … okay." She was right. But he was caught between needing her help and needing to keep her away from Kondracki – and wanting her close. Like now.

She listened to him talk about JK, but he wasn't revealing anything new and there was something he wasn't sharing. She decided to push.

"I want to talk about Zofia's ownership. Let's order lunch and you fill me in before you go back to your sessions."

Talking too much about Zofia is not a good idea. Besides, her scantily covered sexiness had impaired his ability to think. "Victoria, Victoria ... let's talk tonight. Talking about Zofia is a can of worms, and when – "

"Can of worms?"

"No, no." He got up and walked away from the table. "A figure of speech. Lot of crap ... can't wrap my head around it right now." How he handled Zofia would lead to how he handled JK and he needed leverage on both if he was to protect his secret, a secret either one might reveal. Victoria must not know. Not yet. He came back to the table, stopping a few feet short, his rock-like presence casting a shadow over her. He said. "Zofia is weak. Have to handle her with kid gloves. Get to her before he does."

She stood up. "There's something you're not telling me about her father. About her." The conversation was getting heated, and so was she. Her heat was double-sided, frustration and arousal. "Listen, no one knows a woman better than another woman. You need to tell me about her." She held his eyes. "A woman's intuition can tell whether nothing is nothing or she really does know something."

He slapped his hand on the glass table. "Damn it Victoria! What don't ya' get about nothing." He'd startled her. He saw a flash of fear cross her eyes. He spun away from her.

She said. "What *you* don't get ... I'm responsible for the money in this deal. And that's not nothing. Remember ... you report to me."

He tried to control his toxic mix of emotions. He turned. "Why the hell would I report to you about my ex-lawyer when I know her, and her father. And you don't." His eyes were fiery. "I don't want to talk about her. Not now. Not – "

"Now might be all there is if we're going to save this deal. If talking about her helps, then we're talking."

"I don't want her to come between us … I mean … I just – "

"Sorry." She had no idea why she said sorry. But she was thrown off when he said, *I don't want her to come between us.* He blinked. The anger wasn't gone but there was something else. The tautness in his face receded. But there was still turmoil. Frustration? Need?

He reached across the emotions tumbling between them and held her shoulders.

His strength was daunting. But not frightening. His grip was demanding. She leaned back against the glass table.

He saw it in her eyes, a struggle between toughness and fear. He'd frightened her. *I never want to frighten you, hurt you.* She stood before him, dressed in next to nothing and looked like the innocent university student she used to be. That's all he saw. Beautiful innocence. That he'd dragged into his god-awful world of big trouble, big secrets.

She didn't want to fight. She released all pretense at toughness and felt a change ripple through him. Conflicting emotions crumbled, and his energy discharge came in a shudder. He was vulnerable, at risk, standing in front of her – the real Yale Walters. Her resistence melted, apprehension turning to compassion.

Her serenity beckoned him. His hands slipped down her slender arms, grasping her tiny waist and lifting her onto the table. He stepped closer. "You should never be sorry. Never – "

"She could never come between us?"

The moment was instinctive. Mandatory. Her heart commanded her body. Her eyes closed. Then opened. This time she wanted to remember the moment, the connection to the indomitable spirit of Yale Walters.

Controlled by the most exquisite, erotic woman he'd ever known, he eased between her legs as naturally as the waves rolling up on the beach. He whispered, "I need a condom."

"I don't care." She didn't know why she said it but truly didn't care.

He took her mouth. Tongues urgent.

Forceful hands pushed her shorts off and every nerve-ending exploded as she felt her hot skin against the cool table. She yanked her T-shirt off and wrapped her arms around his neck as she sank into the scent of his skin. Kissing. Biting. Intoxicated. Insatiable. Biting. Biting. Biting.

His hands slipped under her tight, bare bottom, forcing their heat together. He squeezed. Hard. She moaned. Harder. He felt her arms leaving him, her breasts moving away as she reclined on the table, her long, lithe legs rising to rest on his shoulders. To welcome him.

Her nerves raged, her body flared and her anticipation throbbed at the fulcrum of her being.

He ran his hand up her long, inner leg into her moisture, inflaming her.

Her arms, hands, fingernails pulled him to her. Her legs forced him forward and her hips lifted her depths to him.

He pushed his molten arousal deep into her pulsating wetness. Hard. Hot. One with her.

She relinquished everything, shattering into ecstasy. Again, she didn't remember where he'd taken her. Or how long they were there. But this time, an indelible imprint had been left in her body … and in her mind. Maybe her heart?

"Incredible …" was all he could manage. He never wanted to leave the moment.

She allowed long, slow breathes to drift between her lips as she eased back into reality, wondering where his reality might be.

She deliberately stepped from the shower first, leaving him soaking in the hot water because she was stirring again and felt weak-kneed. She wrapped a towel around herself and sat on a stool in the corner of the bathroom, watching his magnificent body through the glass. Her world had just been turned upside down, and it looked wonderful from where she was. Extraordinarily beautiful.

From this moment forward, everything would be different.

59

CHAPTER SEVEN

Throughout the afternoon Victoria struggled to focus but he was in 'go mode.' He printed a pile of documents and spread them across the table – the same table they'd just consummated their fantasy on. Every time they were close or passed, he touched her, which would have precipitated another torrid encounter except they'd taken each other, again, when he came out of the shower. On the counter.

He didn't go back to the afternoon meetings and they chatted about, well … just about everything. They laughed and stumbled over each other's words. She said, "If only I hadn't been so stupid the other night in your office – "

"You left me sky-high."

"Yeah but you made up for it at thirty-thousand feet in the sky yesterday."

"Thirty-two thousand."

"It felt like a hundred and thirty-two."

He leaned in. "Want to try for higher?"

She turned her cheek. "Stop it. We've got work to do." She slipped out from under him and reached for her water bottle. Her inner heat was a touch away from demanding him, again. *How difficult is it going to be around this magnificent man … to remain an independent woman?*

He'd agreed to go over everything, and as she immersed herself in her love of high finance the exhilaration of working with the man she'd only fanatsized about a few days ago was now an even bigger distraction. From afar he'd been a dream, now he was her reality. Now, it wasn't just about the love of money, it was … *love? Or something like it? Would it be a dream come true or a nightmare?* In a blink, they'd gone from long-drawn-out, controlled resistance to out-of-control hedonism. As she stacked papers on the glass table she saw her reflection and paused. *Don't get ahead of yourself Dyson.*

They worked hard, kissed often and somehow avoided using the bed or table for anything but paper and laptops. What they found was troubling and what he told her was frightening. His story about Kondracki and the risk to the deal was a tough blow to absorb, and despite colliding emotions – money, love, love, money – trust was still the elephant in the room.

• • •

Despite the threat of JK, and contrary to business instincts, she advanced the second hundred-million so they could close the deal. It was a risky proposition and Carl Kennor might not agree but she'd face that when the time came. *Am I doing this for love or money?*

"Hey beautiful, look at this."

He was sitting at the table scanning his computer. She put her laptop aside and got up from the sectional sofa. "What's up?" He didn't look up. Didn't acknowledge her until she was standing next to him. His screen saver was a picture of him on horseback up in the mountains wearing a Stetson and looking like a real cowboy, her cowboy.

He hit a key and pointed at the screen. "Look."

She felt his arm slip around the inside of her leg and a strong hand squeeze her calf. When he nestled his elbow between her legs and nudged her warmth, she went wet.

"This is the agreement Zofia drew up and – "

"I can't hear a word you're saying … you're a naughty distraction."

"You're a talented woman. Can't you do two things at once?" He pressed his elbow slightly. "You asked what's up. I'm responding

"And?"

"Think you have an out. It's complicated. But doable."

"Tell me."

She pouted. "Make me."

He jammed his hands on his hips and dropped his voice to a low command. "Ms. Dyson. You might be in charge of finances but all the money in the world won't stop me if you don't wipe that sexy-ass pout off your face. Either you tell me or – "

"Or what?" She exaggerated the pout. She gasped as he swept her off the floor like a feather, cradling her full-length in his arms.

"Or I'll make your body and heart betray that brilliant mind of yours and you won't have another lucid thought for at least an hour." He marched into the master bedroom, stepped up to the bed and held her over it. "Gonna tell me?"

"I've lost my voice." She frowned instead of pouting. "All I can do is scream." And once again their love-making screamed out across the humid Caribbean evening as they consumed each other.

While he was showering, she curled up, lingering in the moment. *I never thought I'd see the view from this bed. How things change ... maybe we need to change the rules?*

Emerging from the bathroom he said, "That's it. Now we need to take care of Ms. Apogee. We're gonna solve this."

She jumped up, standing naked in the middle of the bed. "You bet Captain. What are my orders?"

"Get some damn clothes on or we'll never leave this room." He turned and left.

She found him in the war room on his laptop. She explained the loop hole she'd found in the agreement that might allow him to leverage Zofia into selling her shares in Xcryption, independent of JK.

"It's worth a try," he said.

He was on and off the phone the rest of the night, talking to Bernie Solomon, Gerry Whitney and people from the Pentagon.

She had to discipline herself not to keep looking at him as he moved around and touched her when he passed. Over and over she marveled at his physique, his energy, his mind. And now his heart – at least part of it. He stepped in from the balcony where he'd been contemplating the pounding waves. "The first problem with Zofia is that despite her tough lawyer façade, she's a chicken-shit. JK hollowed out his little girl, turned her into an empty shell with a fake persona. I've got to keep her away from that domineering ass until the deal closes. If I can reach – "

"I just got a text from Andrea. Says JK has people looking for his daughter. Haven't found her yet."

"Shit. She'll be running scared. Gotta get to her." He called. "Zofia. It's me. Pick up … pick up …." He tried another number, same message. "Shit." He looked at Victoria. "Wonder where'd she'd go? Or – "

His phone rang. She always thought his phone ring was pretty blatant. *Money* by Pink Floyd. Especially since he'd edited it using the lyrics, 'Money … it's a crime.' She loved the song, but it was a bit much on a phone.

"Zofia, thanks for calling back. Where are you?"

She couldn't avoid the pang of jealousy. He was a little too syrupy as he rattled on about her getting away from her dad and where she might go.

"Not your Fifth Avenue condo, not your sisters, not the Hamptons … none of your usual spots…." He snapped his fingers. "What about here?"

"What?" slipped from Victoria's lips. He was so engrossed he didn't hear her. Or didn't acknowledge her. *Was he serious? After what they'd just shared?*

He yammered on, trying to convince her. "Think about it. I'll call you back in five minutes." He hung up and hit another number.

Victoria interjected. "You mean here? Grenada?"

"Garen, sorry it's late. Can you have wheels up in an hour?" No.

I'm not going. Want you to fly back to New York and get someone. Bring her here. You remember Zofia Gorka? I'll have her at the terminal for 8 am." He listened. "Well, I know you can persuade some Grenadian to get outta bed and fuel her up – whatever it cost."

He hung up. "Here. Face to face. That's the way to convince her. I can – "

She suppressed her distaste for having the ex-lawyer, ex-lover here. "What guarantee do you have she'll agree?"

"I can convince her one-on-one."

"I mean at the airport in the morning." She coughed. "Didn't you tell her to think about it? Even though Garen is already on his way?" Jealousy was spinning the questions. She noticed Zofia's number was a one-number touch.

"Zofia."

He spoke softly but was now all business. Firm. Direct. Compelling. But still a little too charming. *Do some ex-lovers never go away?*

"Garen's fueling the plane as we speak … because I assumed you'd see the light. You know I need your help … Yes, yes, I know the jam you're in. It's not easy. And risky. I understand." He listened. "I know, I know … you're right. But you and I've always been there for each other. You know he's wrong. And this isn't the first time. Remember when we…."

Victoria laid on the bed, trying to distance herself from her rising resentment. Listening to him convince her to cross her ruthless father was necessary, but that didn't change the reality. His charm toward her was like a pointy stick in the eye. She needed peanut butter.

He said, "Zofia, thank you so much. You're a doll. I owe you. Garen'll be there. Wheels up at eight."

She purposely stayed on the bed, elbow on the pillow, head on hand. Jealousy fomenting. "So?"

He dialed another number. "Bernie … sorry about the time.

Zofia is going to do it. Need those documents asap. She'll be here tomorrow … yes, here. Grenada. By noon."

She said nothing.

He looked at her, not so much with a smile but a confirmation. "Good. Almost solved. She gets it. She's smart. Always has been. Just frightened. Be here by noon tomorrow."

"I heard." Then with sarcasm. "Been in the room all the time." *In case you didn't notice.* What she did notice was he was insensitive to her feelings. He'd just won a battle and looked like he was accepting a trophy – his trophy ex-lover – for himself, not the team.

He paced and talked. "I can get her to see the reality of that bastard. I'm sure she'll agree once we walk her through the whole business. And if I have to, I'll use the loophole in the agreement. Just have to handle her right."

You mean the loophole I found? The idea of Zofia being here, in the same room where they'd been intimate, where their love might be flourishing. It didn't sit well. "So...?"

He glanced at her. "So?"

"You gonna tell me all about it?"

"You heard, it's – "

"I didn't hear *her.*"

"Do I sense irritation? A problem?"

She said, "Remember? Openness? Everything on the table – "

"Geez Victoria." He moved toward her, his eyes taking her in. "Is that a hint of jealousy behind those baby blues?" As he sat on the edge of the bed, he put his hand on her hip. "I like that you're jealous. Because I can wash it all away in a matter of seconds." He kissed her. It washed over her. Jealousy left, desire entered. Then he stopped.

"Mr. Charm. Charming all the women."

He extracted himself from her jealous web and pulled her up off the bed.

Her groan was more disappointment than complaint.

They went back to work. She reworked the financials to accommodate an extra ten-million-dollar payment that he was proposing for Zofia, and he figured out how to protect them from JK's response, which would be unpredictable and dangerous.

• • •

Zofia Gorka was not what Victoria expected. From the moment she stepped out of the limousine her attitude reeked of condescending emptiness. She obviously came from money, lived with money and as far as Victoria was concerned could go right back to all that money. But she was attractive, in a glamor-magazine, kind of way. All dolled up, just like Vogue says she's supposed to dress … and pout. It was the kind of conceited pout you see on runway models, empty, dripping in phoniness and wanting to be someplace else. How did he get caught up in *that*?

As he greeted her in the circular driveway, Victoria stood watching from the back of the open-air, lobby. She wondered how he could appear so comfortable with this overdressed, look-how-rich-I-am woman? How could they have been a thing? She held onto, *maybe they weren't.*

Zofia offered a hand. "This must be Victoria?"

Who does she think she is, offering her hand as if she was a queen expecting her subject to kiss it? And who wears a stupid floppy hat and a too-tight dress in this humidity? Dress must have cost a small fortune. She shook the hand, firmly. "Zofia." That was all she was going to say. But then discomfort nudged her into social nicety. "How was the flight?"

"Marvelous. Don't you just love his new jet." She touched his arm and smiled. "Of course, was my first flight on his new Gulfstream, but we've had others."

She cursed herself for asking. There was no way she was having a superficial cat fight with this woman.

She said, "I've heard so much about you," as she looked around to see who else might be watching her.

Bullshit.

He interrupted the tension. "Let's get you settled in. Lunch, the three of us, half hour?"

Victoria said, "Meet you there." She turned and walked away knowing Zofia's eyes were all over her. *Eat your heart out.* Despite the nagging question of how he might have been interested in this rich-bitch lawyer, and how the three of them would feel in the same room, she felt better, in a catty kind of way, knowing this woman was nothing like her.

He was standing behind Zofia, watching her watch Victoria. It was odd. The past and the present, in the same place. He didn't like it. But had to see it through. His gaze followed every inch of Victoria's tall, graceful, movements, until she disappeared beyond the flamboyant trees. The contrast between the two women was not only visual, it was visceral. He'd always known the camouflaged emptiness of Zofia, but had ignored it when they first met because she was striking, in a rich elegant way. And a good lawyer. But no sense of self. No depth. She was smart but not Victoria-smart. And not Victoria-beautiful. They were night and day, darkness and sunshine. Zofia was as unnatural as her blonde hair and all the glitz and glamor that goes with money. Victoria was a real blonde, svelte, understated, quiet and all-natural. Zofia spent a fortune on makeup and he assumed botox and a boob-job were already on the calendar of some world-renowned plastic surgeon. Her need for attention caused her to overdress, overact and over accentuate every social norm. Although they'd spoken from time to time and met regarding this deal, she was nothing more than a distant memory to him, like a manikin in a window.

The lunch was going as well as could be expected. They got past the fluffy stuff and onto business. He made sure there was no ambiguity. He, and by extension, Victoria and Kennor Capital, needed Zofia's cooperation.

Zofia wasn't fully engaged, often distracted by the waiter or people around the pool or by the wind blowing her hair. And she paid no attention to Victoria, acknowledging her only in an oh-you-too manner. But as long as this rich-bitch agreed to sign over her company shares, she didn't give a damn. Yale's focus was on Zofia but under the table he frequently pressed his leg against hers. Lovingly firm.

"Zofia. For now, let's leave it at that. Think it over for a couple of hours." He pointed at the pool. "Get some sun and relax. Then come to my suite for drinks. Six. Then dinner with Victoria and I."

She dabbed the napkin to her lips, managed a half-smile and left, never glancing at Victoria.

"What do you think?"

"About her? You and her? How you did – "

"Victoria. Don't go there." He waggled a friendly finger.

"Sorry. Just don't like the woman."

"Me either. But we have to – "

"I know, I know. But why do I feel like I've been slimed? She's an irritating mix of arrogance and insecurity, hiding behind a phony smile. She never even looked at me until – "

"Don't let her get to you. She means nothing to – "

"You know that octopus in the aquarium in your room?" All she got was a deadpan stare. "You know, the slimy, pretty-but-ugly, eight-legged, sucking bag that looks like a scrotum? Well … I nicked named it Zofia."

"Stop it. This isn't about her, it's – "

"Easy for you to say … Mr. Charm. But I'm the third wheel as far as she's concerned. She's all over you like a teenage slut … shit, you'd think this was some high school reunion or – "

"Victoria – "

"I know … money, money. It's all about the money. But she doesn't get it. I'm the one writing her a ten-million-dollar check …

not you. She should be kissing my ass, not yours … and you sure look like you're enjoying it." *I shouldn't have said that.*

"What the hell does that mean?"

"If she touches you one more time I think I'm going to throw up."

"I'm doing this for us, not – "

"When she touched your cheek and said you were 'so thoughtful …' I damn near threw my glass of wine at her fuckin' head, she – "

"Enough! You're better than this, you don't need to stoop to – "

"What? Stoop where? Down to her weak-assed, no scruples. Playing high school jealousy. She still thinks she's the prom queen, the hottest chick in school, the one every guy wants. But she's empty, just a little woman with a big bank account. And an ex-client, ex-lover, to play with." *Shouldn't have said that … but he didn't flinch. Or deny it.* "Well … not on my account. You handle her, you meet with her. You don't need me." She stopped. Either because she was out of breath or she'd gone too far. He didn't say a word. "Well?"

He looked calm. "Well … nothing. Say what you gotta say. I understand how you feel, you – "

"Don't patronize me. I'm not making this shit up. You know how noxious she is. She's doing this to get in your good graces, to make you owe her, be obligated to her. Keep a connection to you. I know women like her, especially when big money is involved."

"What women?"

"You know, women. Ex-wives, lovers, looking for their pound of flesh. Female Shylocks who live in the shadows of the past and come out every now-and-then to haunt their exs. In this business – you now – wealthy men curse the chains past women tie them up with, especially when there's a new woman in the picture. The exs always come out then. I've seen it time and time again and – "

"And you think Zofia is a threat to us." He took her hand. "You're not jealous, you're afraid."

He was right. She was afraid. Her head was pounding. And

she'd been unaware of her pent-up feelings until they burst out.

"Let's go to the room."

The minute they entered, he opened his arms and she slipped into them like a soothing bath. Her head rested against his unshakeable chest and bubbling emotions subsided.

He hugged harder, "My Victoria."

Not until she's out of your life.

CHAPTER EIGHT

They went to work in the war room. She put the numbers together for the lawyers to draw up Zofia's agreement and he called Bernie and Gerry Whitney to get the final documents sent. He attended two afternoon meetings. She would have gone to the pool but wasn't going to risk bumping into rich-bitch, so she stretched out on the balcony. He came back just after five.

He waved at the ocean. "There's a beautiful beach and ocean out there and we've hardly looked at. I'll make drinks." He poured two, very dry martinis. It was a quiet, just-the-two-of-them, moment. He'd stripped down to his undershorts and she could only stare at his long, muscular body stretched out in the afternoon sun. *Can lasting happiness emerge from overwhelming sexual desire?*

• • •

She should not have been surprised at Zofia's entrance. Her jacket must have cost thirty-grand. A beaded and embroider, three-quarter sleeve, impeccably tailored jacket with a V-neckline and straight hemline that hung perfectly over her not-so-perfect hips. It was exquisite. But totally unsuitable, unless the only point was to say, 'I'm rich.'

The plan was to have a drink and sign the papers and then talk over dinner about where she could go to avoid the threat of her father. The problem started when Victoria took charge, sitting at the table to go over the agreement. Zofia's irritation was obvious. Yale ignored them, working on his laptop on the sofa. She grilled Victoria on every little detail and constantly interrupted with, "Well, when Yale and I worked on this …" or calling over to him, "Do you agree with this?" For Victoria, years of dealing with wealthy, egotistical clients helped control her aggravation, but it was getting under his skin.

"We don't need to relive the past and if Victoria says that's it, that's it." He got up and made a second round of drinks.

Zofia turned to him. "As a lawyer I shouldn't be doing this you know – just saying. I'm going along with it – "

"You're doing it as his daughter, not a lawyer," he said. "Big difference."

"Still a nasty move on my father and – "

"Damn it Zofia. You have no idea what nasty is. What could happen if – "

"Don't lecture me big boy." She looked at him. "You need me more than I need you. And if my father – "

"Exactly! Your father. The epitome of nasty."

Victoria watched. His anger was surfacing. Her jealousy relishing it.

Zofia said, "If he knew what I was doing right now. If he knew what – "

"Geez, don't be so stupid, if – "

"Stupid?"

"Naïve … I mean naïve. You know him."

"I know you. This is all about you. Always has been. Big tough Yale. Gotta prove he can conquer the mountain. Be a billionaire. Put everything at risk, to go where he shouldn't, flirt with the wild side, do whatever it takes … just to prove that he can. To hell with the consequences. To hell with my feelings." She glanced at Victoria. "And to hell with her. You, Miss Beauty Queen, are just another of his conquests."

He was still at the counter so his shouting wasn't as shattering as his glare. "Consequences? You don't know shit about consequences.

Never have. Never will. If you did, you'd sign those goddamn papers and run. And leave Victoria out of this. Or – "

"Or what?"

"Or I'll toss your ass on a commercial flight and cancel the whole fuckin' deal."

My sentiments exactly, thought Victoria. *Yikes ... he'd do that for me?*

Zofia's phone rang, playing Sinatra's "New York, New York."

He yelled from across the room, "Don't answer."

Too late.

"Yes?"

Sitting next to her, she could hear a growling voice. But couldn't make out the words.

As Zofia listened, he crossed the room and set the drinks on the table. He stood listening, tension rising in his strapping frame.

Zofia said. "I hear you ... What do you mean, where am I? I don't have to tell you every time I leave town – But Daddy ..."

Yale's eyes leaped. He knocked over the drinks as he pulled the phone from her hand and hit end.

Zofia let out a whimpering yip. "What the fuck was – ?"

"He can track you. Locate you." The phone rang. He ignored it.

Glaring, she stared at the gin all over her extravagant jacket. "Look what the hell you've done. What's your problem? I didn't say anything. Was only a couple of minutes."

Victoria hid her grin.

He barked. "You better hope that jacket is the only damage from that call."

She looked like she didn't know whether to explode or cry, and it wasn't clear if it was from the messed-up jacket or fear.

"Zofia, I don't have to remind you of past ghosts. Your father's ghosts."

Victoria was silent as he recounted a story about one of JK's condominium developments in Edgewater, New Jersey. He reminded her about how the project was the only one being built during a union strike. There was absolutely no concrete delivered to any project, in New Jersey or Manhattan, except to JK's projects. "And I don't have to remind you who controls the Teamsters union and the supply of ready-mix concrete. Mobsters. Your ol'man's buddies, Tony Delano and Fats Cercone. Remember how a few of the workers on a competitor's condo picketed, protesting the strike. And how one of them, the leader, disappeared a few months later, without a trace. I'd bet if your father had any feelings – and he doesn't – then that man's ghost would be haunting him to this day. That's who you're up against, face it or not."

Victoria went to the bathroom.

He was still simmering but spoke calmly. "Your father knows I am here, in Grenada, trying to finalize the deal with the Pentagon. Like I explained, he wants to sell Xcryption to a third world country." He exhaled. "He controls Xcryption but if you sell your shares to Apogee, he loses control because when we have a thirty-three percent stake, he must have our approval for any sale. He always knew he had control of you so wasn't worried." He jammed his finger on the papers in front of her "That's why you have to sign these."

She looked defeated.

Victoria decided to push while she was vulnerable. "Let's get the paperwork finished. My firm will buy you out, plus give you an additional payment of $10 million." She put a pen in front of her and turned the pages marked for signing. With every signature, she pushed this woman further and further into the past. *Because there ain't enough room in this guy's world for the two of us.*

He admired how quickly Victoria got the signatures, jumping in when she did. They'd overcome a huge hurdle. Now he could turn his attention to the mounting threat of JK. Because if he tracked his daughter to Grenada, not only was the Pentagon deal in jeopardy, they all were. He then made an announcement that was music to

Victoria's ears. "Zofia, you can have dinner on your own. Or I can order you room service. Or get the limo to take you to one of the great restaurants on the island. But Victoria and I have a whole night's work ahead of us."

Victoria held back another grin.

The woman pouted like a five-year old. "I'll bet you do."

He walked her to the door and she obediently left. But not before getting one more hug from him. Victoria noticed she lingered in the hug, almost not wanting to let go. He allowed it. She never said good-bye.

"Well done beautiful." He took her in his arms. The upwelling washed away the dirt, grime and fear. Despite the impending danger, she was excited about the work ahead and the ex-whatever's departure added to her lightness.

Not moving her head from his chest, she asked, "Do you really think JK could trace her here?"

"Absolutely."

"Why? I mean if she – "

He leaned back and reassuringly held her shoulders. "He'll stop at nothing. My bet, if he finds out she's here … he'll come. Or send some very bad dudes. For a few hundred million, murder-for-hire is not beyond this guy." He kissed her forehead. "With the thirty-three percent at risk, no telling what he'll do." He kissed her again. "We have work to do. What was your father's favorite saying?"

She smiled. "First the necessary, then the useful, then the pleasant."

They worked well into the night and at one point, their bleary eyes met and acknowledged exhaustion was winning. After a hug and a few sensual touches, they fell into bed and sleep erased the clashing emotions of love and fear.

• • •

Whether it was the mounting fear or the residue from Zofia, in the quiet light of dawn she could not control her urge to make love to him as she spooned his sculpted body. But she had to resist. He needed his sleep. She snuck out of bed and tipped toed into the kitchen to make coffee and green tea. Thirty minutes later he was up and they were reviewing spreadsheets before room service delivered breakfast. After yakking and laughing over breakfast, they got back to work but she no longer could suppress her needs. Female instinct pushed her to reclaim her man – now – now that the princess-bitch was gone. As he talked on the phone, she planted herself confrontationally in front of him, hands on hips, breasts pushed out.

He grinned at her I'm-in-charge stance and kept talking. She didn't move. He kept smiling and his eyes turned to intrigue.

"Okay," he said into the phone. "Call you back in a few minutes."

The second he poked the screen, she poked his abs. Hard. "Mr. Walters will be busy for the more than the next few minutes. He might be late returning your call."

"What happened to 'the necessary' and 'the useful?'"

She sparkled with mischief. "This is necessary, for me. And hopefully useful for you. And it's out-of-this-world with pleasure." She plunked her hand on his chest and pushed him onto the bed.

"Whoa. Go directly to the pleasant … do not pass Go, do not collect two hundred dollars – or is that two-hundred-million?" He chuckled. "I was always good at Monopoly but didn't know it could be a sex game."

"So you think this is a game do ya' buster?" She was wearing one of his blue shirts and unbuttoned it. As she took her phone out of the pocket, it rang. It was Carl Kennor. "Shit!"

"Hey, no timeouts," he shouted from his prone position. "Shut that damn thing off."

"Gotta take this." She turned and walked to the center of the room. "Carl – "

He hauled himself off the bed, flashed her a big frown and went to his laptop.

"I understand … but there's more to it than – " She listened to what was obviously a one-way conversation. "Yes, he's fully cooperative. We're on the same page and … I understand. Carl, it's irrelevant – " Why would you ask?

He watched as her voice became tense.

"Carl, I've got this. Trust me." She was adamant. "Understood. Talk tomorrow." She jammed her finger on the screen.

She inhaled and turned toward him, her shirt still unbuttoned.

"What's up partner?"

"Aaaah … Carl and his usual control-freak, bullshit." She plunked her butt on the edge of the table. "He dug into Kondracki's background and doesn't like it. He knows most of what we know. And is threatening to pull out and – "

"He can't. It's too late to – "

"He's not. Just threatening. I told him I was handling it. In fact, might be good he's in on it. Has a lot of resources if we need them."

She was talking a good story but her face said otherwise. "Victoria … something you're not telling me?"

"I will, I will." She looked at the floor, then back. The brilliance had faded. "He asked if I was sleeping with you – in his usual tactless way. I actually never – "

He retorted. "I'd like to say it's none of his fuckin' business but under the circumstances … it's complicated."

"I never answered his question."

"Is that when you told him it was irrelevant?"

"Is that what I said?"

"Yeah." He walked over and took her hands. "It's a good thing. The fact that you and I are in sync – in every way – will be far better than if we were at each other's throats." He bent down and kissed her neck. "But maybe we should back off for now. Ease Carl's jitters. Tell him something … that we've decided to separate the money from the personal … and sleep in our respective rooms … for now. Tell him it was a one-time thing."

She couldn't feel her heart. It was a tiny spec receding into the void as she listened to what sounded like a dispassionate rationale. *Sleep in our respective rooms*?

He continued. "It would only be for a week. Until we close. Not easy. But we could summon our iron-will. Rewrite your rules. Do whatever it takes to close the deal … in the name of money. What do you think?"

She didn't have a thought. Or a feeling – except numbness. It felt just like the night in his office when she abandoned him with her goddamn iron-will. But she no longer had it. He'd robbed her of it.

He saw in her face everything he needed to know. "Oh god … what am I saying. Shit!" He slapped his forehead. "Now it's me being stupid. To even think I could be apart from you is …" He frowned. "Fuckin' money makes me crazy." He put his hands on her shoulders. "Forgive my stupidity. We're not giving up *us* for Kennor or Kondracki or any amount of money."

She could feel her heart again, its rhythm returning. But still frightened.

He kissed her. Not heatedly, just reassuringly.

His kiss was her security blanket. She leaned against his chest. Carl didn't frighten her, and she was more than prepared to stand up to him, often had, but the thought of being apart from Yale scared the hell out of her. This little episode showed her that the conflict between big money and personal emotions was beyond her sex-rules. It could now jeopardize important things in her life. Like her career. Like him. Hearing his beating heart soothed her jagged edge. He'd be her rock. Since her dad had passed, it was the one thing independent Victoria had not had, a rock. She looked into his eyes. "I didn't answer Carl's question about sleeping together. But he knows."

"Good. He's smart. Knows both of us. Has faith in you. He'll see the value in our total partnership. So let's wrap up the biggest fuckin' deal in your career – and mine."

"You're my biggest fuckin' deal, in every way … every inch of you."

He grabbed her by the waist and lifted her over his head as her unbuttoned shirt brushed across his beaming smile. "Let's take the world on Beautiful."

She let out a sound that was a mix of laughter, joy and whoopee."

He hung her over his shoulder and headed for the bedroom when there was a knock at the door. He hesitated. "It's her." He slowly put her down. "Gotta get it."

Her rising heat crashed in a cold avalanche as she buttoned her shirt.

Zofia pushed into the room. "My father has been calling all night. Two, three times an hour. If I – "

"You didn't answer?"

"If I can't get my sleep, you know – "

"You didn't answer?"

"Of course not. But if he – "

"Zofia, Zofia." He guided her to a chair.

Victoria went to the bedroom. When she returned, he was consoling her – a little too compassionately according to her jealous, inner voice.

He said. "The fact that he keeps trying to reach you suggests he doesn't know where you are. That's good. But I think we should decide where you go until this is over. I'll fly you wherever you want. Can't be anywhere he'd look. Not your sisters or any of your usual haunts – Monaco, London, certainly not New York. Could be a hotel or resort, under an assumed name. But stay away from friends and relatives."

She looked lost. "Where?"

"The sooner the better," he said. "I have a pied-à-terre in Phoenix, it's small. We have an office there too, I can have someone keep an eye on you."

Victoria said. "I have a place in New Mexico. A ski chalet. Small too. But comfortable. Only use it in the winter." He raised his eyebrows as if to say, I didn't know you skied. "It's out of the way, in Taos. North of Santa Fe."

"Sounds ideal," he said.

"No way," Zofia spit out. "I'm not going to some god-forsaken place and live in a ski shack." She stared at Victoria. "Thanks anyway." The condescension was thick. "Not interested … no offense."

"No offense taken."

He chafed. "Zofia, go and pack. I'll come up with a safe place. Wheels up at noon."

"Fine. You got want you wanted and now it's get rid of me. Typical." She marched out.

As the door closed he said, "Good riddance."

Noon couldn't come soon enough. Every time this woman was around, she needed a shower.

He was sending emails so she went ahead and showered on her own, hoping his not joining her was because he was busy, not a residual effect of Carl's influence. She was still drying her hair when he stepped into the shower in his gloriously chiseled nakedness.

Fuck Carl. Fuck the money.

CHAPTER NINE

As they sat down to lunch with the Pentagon people, he touched her arm, pointed to his watch, gave her a knowing smile and said, "Wheels are up." He rolled his eyes and her heart floated into the Caribbean sky.

It was as a delightful lunch with Justine Cameron and Major Adams and they were in agreement with the terms of the contract, agreeing to sign next Wednesday in Washington. She couldn't have been happier. Here she was on a beautiful island, watching her magnificent man at the peak of his game and partnering with him in what would be the biggest deal of her life. Her dad would've been proud.

Part of her delight was that he'd put Zofia on his jet and sent her to Toronto. Apogee had an office there and he arranged for her to stay at a friend's summer home on an out-of-the-way Canadian lake called Muskoka. *Thank god she was gone.* And they'd heard nothing more about JK. Bernie and Andreas' PIs reported they'd located him at his home in New Jersey.

Throughout lunch she saw two sides of him. All business, charming, persuasive and confident. At the same time, the mischievous flirt touched her under the table with his feet, legs and hand. She was experiencing the relentless entrepreneur stocking prey and the wild-side adventurer stocking her. At first, his feet played with her, sending sensations up her legs, then his hand ventured up her thigh and she struggled to pretend she was listening to the conversation. It was hard to believe he could carry on the conversation while playing with her. Yesterday, he'd said he'd like to have sex with her in a public place, suggesting the elevator, the pool, the ocean. Was he thinking that now? The pool? The lunch table? *I could meet him in the men's washroom.* At one point, as he was talking to Justine about sailing the Caribbean he said, "… there is nothing like sailing into a safe harbor when you're in the middle of a storm…." At that moment, with artful grace, he slipped his hand between her legs and his long fingers momentarily pressed against her. And then he was gone, chatting about something else. *He can play with me for the rest of my life.*

Victoria was at his side, the Pentagon was onside, and Zofia was gone. He felt good. But JK wasn't gone. He motioned to the waiter. "Another bottle of Chardonnay…." He turned to Major Adams. "When do you guys fly back?"

"Sunday morning. Too damn early. I think the flights at 7:30."

"7:40," said Justine.

"How'd you like to leave with us at a more civilized hour?"

Justine looked inquisitive. "What time does your flight leave?"

He smiled. "When we get there."

They agreed to take the ride on his Gulfstream, but she wondered if Pentagon conflict of interest regulations might apply. She was in charge of the money and should question him, but her heart said, *don't spoil his fun.*

• • •

In the afternoon, he was part of a panel discussion and she decided to attend, to see her man in action. He was mesmerizing. Not just with his presence on stage but with the depth of his knowledge and his ability to articulate complex subjects. She marveled as he held the audience's attention with one hand, and her fantasies in the other. She felt him deep inside her. In addition to the raw physical attraction, he intellectually aroused her and she listened to techie subjects that any other time she would have ignored. After the panel, people milled around, lining up to talk to him. She stood at the back of the room but wanted to go up and drag him backstage and bring to life one of his in-public, sex fantasies. *Probably no different than most of the women in the room.* Instead she did the necessary and went back to the room to revise the financial statements for buying out Zofia. Carl Kennor was going to demand one hell of an explanation as to how she planned to cover the extra ten-million. Even though they had work to do this evening, it came with a large bonus, him. Working next to him was like being a sex addict in a sex emporium, with an open tab.

Her phone rang. He sounded apologetic.

"I have to go to dinner with Major Adams and a bunch of scientists." She heard the sigh. "Got roped into it."

She hoped her response didn't sound like she felt – flat. "Understood. I'll be here. Lots to do."

"I'll get away as soon as I can." He whispered. "Wait for me."

"With open arms."

Still whispering he said, "Open everything …"

"Everything …?" She thought she hung up without even saying good-bye as she spoke to the empty room … "you got it, everything." She sank onto the sofa, basking in fantasy. She could smell him, taste him, feel him … she reveled in opening everything to him. It was ten minutes before she'd cleared her mind and body.

She completed the spreadsheets and then went to her room to get a change of clothes. She was undecided. The coconut-white, satin, midi-slip or the red Teddy. *The coconut-white is appropriate for the tropics.* Had she packed too much sexy underwear? Too many choices? *Good planning Dyson.*

It was after ten when he came through the door. This time she didn't run to him, she walked, slowly, deliberately. With purpose.

He tossed his jacket on the chair. His heart jumped, his smile stretched, his pulse rose. Victoria, framed in the bedroom doorway, was what he imagined an oasis looked like to a man dying of thirst.

She was more beautiful, alluring and sexually beguiling than any woman should be allowed to be. And she was his woman. Here. Before him … in the naughtiest, most erotic underwear.

From fifteen feet away, she felt his inner pounding, the unraveling of his wild side. This was the reason she brought the red Teddy. She loved Teddies, and this was her favorite. It was sheer mesh with a plunging v-line stretching to a thong bottom. Beyond suggestive.

He didn't move, as every muscle went to red alert. But he forced a tempering of his savage need, so his mind could absorb her pure wonderment. Until she moved. Then thoughts gave way to hunger. Without a word, he moved toward her. That's when he noticed the black tote bag over her shoulder. His mind interrupted his erupting body and he cleared his parched throat, "What's in the bag?"

All he got was a wicked grin.

He swept her up with irresistible force. She floated in his uncontained power. He spun her around and around, crossing the living room as if dancing them into a world of ecstasy. He stopped and eased her onto her toes. The fire in his eyes enflamed her inner sanctum.

He murmured. "My angel. My addiction."

"Your sex addiction?"

"Much more."

His desperation pressed into her.

He asked, "What's in the bag?"

It was still over her shoulder. "To be opened in the bedroom." He swooped her up, marched into the bedroom and tossed her, not so gently, on the bed. She was electrified by his aggressiveness. Her arousal magnified. Kneeling on the bed, she pouted and held the bag behind her back.

"Victoria…"

"I don't know. You may not be the bad boy I think you are. I can't be sure. You've never told me what you like and what you don't and – ”

"Are you playing games again?"

"This isn't Monopoly. It's more like hang man. Or hang women."

"If you keep me hanging, I'm not – ”

"I absolutely love how you're hung. And right now, I want to explore every inch of you."

He stepped up next to the raised bed. She gently stroked his hardness. He shuddered. She undid his belt and he did the rest, pushing his pants and underwear to the floor. She watched as he stepped out of them, magnificent in all his incredible, hard glory. His breadth, stature and radiating heat overtook her, tremors shooting through her body. She took him in her mouth.

He convulsed and grabbed her head in his hands. A guttural sound came from somewhere and he arched back, holding her head firmly. "I want all of you...." He pushed her away.

She put the bag in front of him and opened it. "First – ”

He looked in. "Oh my god … you beautiful bitch!"

"You are my sex slave."

He pulled out several strips of fabric and a pair of handcuffs.

She pulled him down on the bed, rolling him onto his back. It was all she could do not to mount him. But she wanted more. "Mr. Walters, put your hands over your head."

She was escalating a tension in his body he'd never experienced before. As she knelt next to him, he craved to touch her. He stroked the soft, delicate hairs on her forearm, ran his hand up over her ever-so-sexy upper arm, along her neck and then slipped a finger into the corner of her mouth. She sucked, then bit. She began to tie his wrists. He wanted to devour her. As she leaned over him he kissed her belly. She involuntarily pushed against him.

She tried to tie his wrists tight but the desire raging inside rushed her and she didn't secure them. She denied her urge to mount his handsome erection and slid down his body, kissing his chest, abs, cock, thighs and feet. Then tied both ankles to the bedposts. He made no sound. She stood at the end of the bed and removed the Teddy. She struggled to go slow, every nerve-ending screaming, *take him, take him….*

His muscles strained. He could have ripped his wrists from the fabric, but wanted the restraint, loved her need to control, to subdue his animal hunger. As she started to straddle him, he waited for her at the intersection of submissiveness and domination. The heat from her inner thighs flooded his groin and the hair that covered her wet folds teased his cock.

She gasped as she lowered herself, deliberately, disciplined, down the length of him, holding his throbbing for a moment, without moving, without a sound. Then constricted her inner muscles.

His massive frame lurched, his powerful hips lifted off the bed.

She pressed her hands into his chest, fingers digging into taut muscles. She moved tantalizingly slow, rhythmically. He tried to thrust. She pushed him down. His wrists strained at the fabric. She sat up straighter. Pressed harder. He thrust, she pushed back, raking nails across his chest, down his abdomen. He ripped his wrists from the fabric, clamping his hands on her shoulders. Forcing down, thrusting up. Her control was giving way to need.

His hands dropped and clenched her bottom, she abandoned control. He took charge. Hard, aggressive, unrelenting. Her swollen channel trembled. She plunged forward, slamming her breasts into his chest, dragging her aroused clitoris hard across his hammering body … and rapture erupted. His sexual quest exploded.

They floated in exhaustion, then began the downward drift into elation, lying silent in their new world. He stirred. She squeezed. He whispered. "You forgot the handcuffs."

She dug her nails into his behind. "Next time."

"Promises, promises …"

Their hearts laughed.

He said, "This is our apogee."

CHAPTER TEN

Victoria spent the morning putting the final numbers in the statements to send to Carl Kennor and then she joined Yale and a group at a poolside, buffet lunch. As they worked their way through the line she whispered, "If this is work, and useful, I'm not sure I can handle the pleasure part."

He smiled but didn't look at her. "You already did."

Major Adams and Justine Cameron approached their table and it was obvious they were concerned about something. Adams said, "We need to talk … now."

Yale was calm. "Somewhere private."

Adams looked at her. "You too Ms. Dyson."

They found an unoccupied meeting room and sat at a small round table. Adam's demeanor was urgent. "My office has been contacted by a lawyer, a lawyer for J.K. Kondracki. Apparently, he's putting a stop to your deal. As of this morning – "

Yale raised a hand.

Her pulse doubled but he seemed unperturbed. Of course, he always presented a stone exterior even when he was churning inside. *Especially when he's tied up.*

He said. "He can't do that. Legally, he's bound by our agreement. What else do you know?"

"Whether he can or can't doesn't matter," said Adams. "If this becomes a legal mess, next week doesn't happen. And if – "

He raised his hand again. "Grant, I understand. And appreciate your position." His eyes drew them both in. "We'll not jeopardize either of you. You've made it clear, Xcryption must be totally in

Apogee's control when you sign the contract. It will be."

She admired his poise. His tall, broad frame sat arrow-straight, steady but relaxed. Face resolute, eyes unwavering. His hands were animated, moving in concert with his words. He let the silence emphasize his point.

Adams sat back. "We know the sale is contingent on our contract, but we need to know, in no uncertain terms, that you can close the deal…. That there'll be financial stability and no legal wrangling."

Justine said. "Deep pockets are needed to finance the demand we'll have."

"If I might." Yale leaned forward. "No one can assure you about the finances better than Victoria …" He held their gaze and moved his hand, putting it on the table in front of her. *Such a strong hand. Commanding. In charge … loving.*

He turned to her. "Let her tell you where we are on that front."

In a split second, she stifled the emotional surge and refocused. "Of course." She inhaled through her first words. "We share this in confidence. Our lawyers haven't completed the paperwork yet … tonight." She explained how buying Zofia's shares gave them control over anything Kondracki might try and do.

He'd pushed his chair back to watch Adams and Cameron as she talked. They were attentive. Engaged. She was good. She reminded him of a lioness on the prowl, protecting the pride. She had an aura of authority and a full grasp of the financial and legal issues. This woman could kick down any glass ceiling – and had.

Later, when they returned to his room, he said, "Shit … I knew it, knew it. This bastard must be stopped." He walked onto the balcony.

She followed. "What if instead of going after JK directly, we go after his client, the country wanting the encryption software. She put her hand on his shoulder. "They may have more to lose."

He put his arm around her waist and pulled her close. She

was comfort and confidence, all in one. "What does my conniving woman have in mind?"

"You mean before you put your arm around me or after?"

"Both. But give me the before first."

"I can't … until there's a little space between us." She reluctantly eased his grip from her waist and holding his hand took him to sit opposite her on two chaise lounges. "Here's what I'm thinking."

As words rolled from her lips, he was enthralled. He picked up a towel and wiped perspiration from his forehead, knowing the heat wasn't just from the morning sun. She explained how well-connected Carl Kennor was in Washington and that there was a possibility that he could contact someone in the State Department who might have some influence on a small, third world country, especially if it was favorable for the Pentagon. He said. "There's a risk Kennor might panic and pull out."

"He doesn't panic."

"I mean … get cold feet. Back out."

She touched his arm. "Possibility. Not a probability. At least not until he's heard me out. Carl loves money more than anything, and he isn't about to risk losing if there's a way out."

He said. "That's plus ten-million, since Zofia signed her shares over last night."

His forearm was hot and sweaty from the sun and it was all she could do to concentrate. "He's in too deep. He'll listen to me." She was trying to convince herself as well as him.

"Your call. You're the boss." *I'd do business with this woman forever.*

"Better to call Carl sooner versus later."

"Agree. Besides, tonight is the awards dinner and dance so let's resolve this now. I want to enjoy you tonight, no distractions."

"Reminds me. I have an appointment at the salon. Gotta look great for my man."

He beamed. "Go ahead. But I doubt they can improve upon perfection."

The afternoon was a flurry of calls to and from lawyers and three calls with Carl Kennor. On the first, Victoria explained the problem, put forward her strategy and asked him to call in a favor at the State Department. His reply was, "I'll get back to you." She was optimistic, Yale pessimistic.

He called back within the hour, saying he'd placed a call and was waiting to hear. He also did what didn't surprise her, requested another pound of flesh from the deal, from Apogee and Yale. He wanted Apogee to pay the additional $10 million going to Zofia and he wanted – demanded – another quarter point on the money Kennor Capital was advancing. She discussed the ten million vehemently and said, "I negotiated that and did not ask him to agree to pay it." Carl responded. "Maybe your personal bias got in the way?" She couldn't argue that.

"Whatever," was all Yale said.

The third call from Carl confirmed the State Department's reply. They'd 'see what might be done. No guarantees.'

She went to the salon feeling a little better. He went for a long run on the beach.

• • •

She got ready for the dinner in her room, where she'd hardly been since arriving. But she wanted to prepare for the evening – for him – on her own. Make it special. Besides she had that adorable, beaded slipdress, the Michael Kors number she'd bought at Bergdorf's. She could never have guessed the six-inch slit on the left thigh would be so perfectly designed for the occasion.

He knocked on her door at six-thirty. When she opened it; he was speechless. Nothing had prepared him. Not the first time, not the red Teddy, not his wildest imagination.

He felt weightless standing in her beauty. He allowed her presence to be etched into his mind and then, without a word, held out his arms. She walked into them. He whispered, "You are absolutely necessary to me."

The dinner was filled with small talk and boring scientific chatter and the boredom was worse because he was next to her and she wanted everybody to vanish. He was attentive but politely so because supposedly they were just business partners, although their secret affection could not be all that secret. By the time dessert came, her physical need for him was at the point of starvation. She wanted to haul him out of there. Then the music started and the room darkened. It was as if they were alone.

"Ms. Dyson, may I have this dance."

He rose in front of her like the hundred-million-dollar man he was. Her Greek god. When he unbuttoned his dark blue jacket, she wanted to slip inside his crisp white shirt and sink her nails into his dense chest. Instead, she just gave him her hand.

He cradled her close, but not too close, trying to make it look as if he was dancing with a business partner. Everyone was watching – gawking at – Victoria. But soon, he couldn't resist. Her body drew him in. *To hell with what people think.*

She let her body become one with him. The music was just there, background to every feeling she'd ever imagined a dance could be. Her insides vibrated as his handsome hardness pressed against her tummy and her black-lace underwear dampened. When the song ended, he whispered, "What are we to do Ms. Dyson?" And then his phone vibrated. It wasn't the kind of vibrator she had in mind.

A low "shit" slipped from his lips. They walked stoically back to the table as he answered the phone. "Have to get this." He seated her and left the ballroom.

As a few minutes became five, then ten, she felt abandon. She made small talk, mostly listening to a scientist and his wife talk about their homes in Portland Maine, Washington and Progreso, Mexico. Her mistake was mentioning she'd once spent a summer in Maine because it opened-up a gushing stream of empty chatter about every antique store and lobster shack between Portland and Bar Harbor. It reminded her of how far her life had come since that torrid summer romance with Kelly. Then her heart quickened as she saw Yale enter the far side of the ballroom. As he got closer, his face was shadowed even though he was smiling for the crowd. He sat and under the table gently squeezed her thigh.

"Sorry folks ... business. Never ends." A bobbing bunch of nattering heads nodded.

She decided to recover the wondrous feelings of their last dance. She touched his arm. "Dance?"

"Ms. Dyson, it would be my pleasure." He took her arm. "But ... unfortunately we can't."

Not only did her smile disappear, so did her inner glow.

He pulled her in with his eyes. "Unfortunately, we have some urgent business to attend to." He turned to the guests. "Ms. Dyson is our CFO and I need her to send some files to our New York office, asap. Hope you'll forgive me for taking her away ... back shortly." He stood, pulling her up.

There was a collective, half-hearted groan from the overdressed, over-stuffed group.

She smiled. "She you shortly."

As they stepped into the hall and turned toward the lobby he started talking. "Bernie called. Private investigator tracked JK. He's up to something. Two unidentified guys visited his home in New Jersey. Spent an hour there. One wore an odd hat or headdress, looked like African garb. Then JK went into Manhattan. Spent couple hours at one of his legal firms. Then met some unsavory associates in Queens. Then had dinner with two other lawyers ... specialty is trust law. Could be about Zofia's trust?

She had trouble keeping up with his long strides. Her tight-fitting, beaded dress was not made for this. *It was made for his undivided attention, not chasing after him.* She tugged on his elbow.

He half-turned and slowed. "Shit … Sorry."

There was no depth in his face. She couldn't read him.

The air-conditioned suite was a relief from the humid air and she plopped onto the sofa while he grabbed a bottle of water from the refrigerator.

She said. "Regardless of what he's doing, he can't change the deal now."

"Don't be too sure. If anybody can – "

"Has he really had people killed?"

He sat next to her, tucked one long, athletic leg under the other, snapped the top off the water and passed it to her. He touched her hair. "I know this man. Diabolical is an understatement. But he's not about to go that far. This involves his family." It sounded hollow.

She took a drink of water and passed the bottle back. He took a swig. *When you drink from the same bottle, it's got to be love.*

"My concern is you. I don't want – "

"Me?"

"There's no need to expose you to him. I can handle him and – "

"Expose me?" She stiffened. "I can handle myself. And anything he might throw at us." She heard her standard, glass ceiling defensiveness speaking. "Besides, we've already cut him out and – "

"Just worried about what he might do to try and find Zofia. If he gets to her, who knows what he could get her to do?"

"You seem upset. Is it her? Don't trust her – "

"I'm fine, fine."

She squeezed his arm. "You're not."

His phone buzzed. "Bernie."

He listened, she watched. His face was gray, eyes dark. She put her other hand on his thigh. He didn't notice. His jaw jutted out. "Bernie. Give the PI my number. Tell him to find out where. Have him call me directly. Immediately."

He hung up and did what he always did when angry. Paced. The news was troubling. The private investigator had overheard JK on his phone as he left a restaurant. All he heard was 'wheels up, nine-thirty.' He suspected the worse. JK was either going to Toronto in pursuit of Zofia or coming to Grenada. Neither was good.

When he was in this mode, it was hard to engage him, but she knew she had to. JK was a problem but as far as she was concerned, financially she had locked him out. Was there something she didn't know? He was more stressed than usual. He'd called Bernie twice in ten minutes and hardly spoken to her. She had to press.

"Yale, I get the gist of what's going on and – "

He was looking into the blackness that stretched to the horizon and didn't turn around. "You think you do. But you don't."

She ignored the dismissiveness. She stopped several feet behind him. She felt the space between them and didn't like it. "I know we have a solid legal and financial position and JK isn't going to upend it now. I also know there's something bothering you that you're not saying. Not sharing and – " She shuddered as he turned. His eyes were glassy, trying to hide behind narrow slits.

"You have no idea. Know nothing about this guy. How dangerous he is. When backed into a corner he's ... knowing how you've screwed him financially ... who knows what he might do."

He seemed to be talking right past her, fixed on something in the future. His phone buzzed. "Who? ... Yes, of course." He listened. "Thanks."

She asked, "Who?"

He paced. "PI says JK's flight plan is Grenada. Wheels were up at 9:30 tonight ... That puts him here around 1:30." He faced her. "I'm going to meet him ... Alone."

She took a slow breath. "No, *we* ... she paused, ... "are going to meet him. We're in this together and – "

"You're going nowhere near this bastard. Not a chance."

"Need I remind you of my responsibilities. I have to deliver this deal on behalf of Kennor Capital and if JK is a threat to our financial investment then I'm going to be there."

He turned and put space between them. "This isn't about your responsibilities, this is about your safety. I won't let you within a mile of this asshole." He locked on her eyes. The blue was as steady and calm as he'd ever seen. "Victoria, trust me. I know what I'm doing."

"I'm sure you do. The problem is, I don't know what you're doing. You say, trust you, but I feel you're not sharing something with me. And won't talk about it … where's the trust in that?"

He turned away and made a call. "Zofia … no, no. Just listen. I need your father's private phone number … no, no. Everything's fine. Just have to … I said, everything is fine.… I need it now … Text it." He hung up and stared at the screen.

She decided to wait for him to respond to her trust question.

He tapped the screen and waited. "JK … Yale here. We need to talk. Not on the phone, face to face … Don't play games with me. I know you're in the air, coming here." He listened. "Call me when you're on the ground. I'll tell you where … Be alone."

Victoria decided it was time to pull rank. She started calmly even though her stomach was in turmoil. And it wasn't the business stress, it was the personal confrontation. She hated it. "Yale. Enough is enough. You can't lone-wolf this. Remember, when it comes to the business, you report to me. And with two-hundred million already on the line, I'm coming to meet JK. And I'm not asking, I'm telling you." She tried to see past the shadows in his eyes and hoped he saw the conviction in hers. She wanted to take his hands but there was a wall of apprehension between them.

"Victoria, Victoria … you don't get it. This isn't about two-hundred million, it's personal, between JK and me. Goes way back. You're being there will make it worse. It won't work. Believe me …" He added, "trust me."

"There you go again with that trust shit." She tried to temper her frustration. "There can be no secrets between us. In business or personal. A partnership is a fragile ship and we are in the same boat. You have to – "

"You're right. This partnership," he pointed a finger between them, "must be pretty fragile if you can't trust me when we're in the middle of a firestorm and I tell you – "

"Just tell me, look me in the eye, and tell me that you're not hiding something from me." Her baby blues blazed. "Come on."

He turned away. "I want trust. And can't get it. You want honesty. And won't believe me. And – "

"See. You can't do it – "

"Bullshit." He was on the edge of yelling. But he wasn't looking at her, he was staring into the distance. Or somewhere?

"Yale, this is not bullshit – unless you're talking about your lack of honesty. How the hell do you expect us to – "

"I guess I don't expect much … I thought – "

"What the hell does that mean?" She heard the fear in her question. And saw his shoulders slump. As he turned profile and walked to sit at the table his silhouette looked like a majestic lion withdrawing from a fight.

She fired at him. "Since when does Yale Walters not expect much? This doesn't have to be like this." She wanted to go to him, but her instincts said, give him some space. Her nerves jangled as she stood still and disobeyed her screaming heart, *go to him, hold him.*

Suppressing his reluctance, he said, "Okay … you can come."

She moved toward him and as he remained sitting, she wrapped her arms around his shoulders. With one strong arm around her hips, he pulled her close.

The space between them warmed but the tension didn't disappear. She sat opposite him and they chatted about what they would do in the meeting with JK. She did not press him about what he wasn't telling her. *Leave it for another day. Tonight will be tough enough.* She was glad he'd conceded to her coming.

She was about to go her room and change when Carl Kennor called. After a lot of listening, she thanked him and hung up. "Good news, bad news."

"Give me the bad first."

"The State Department says JK is dealing with a satellite group out of Somalia. Bad bunch. They're not a hundred percent sure but it's intel's best guess. If it was certain … with hard evidence, they'd have the FBI on it. But they don't have enough yet."

"What kind of proof?"

"Didn't say."

"I bet we could provide proof. What, with Bernie's files, and the PI's photos of the visitors at JK's house … hell, maybe we can take JK down?"

She felt his excitement. "Could be leverage."

"Could keep him away from Major Adams and Justine, which is the main reason he's coming here. All we have to do is mention Somalia and they'll never speak to him. That might stop him from blowing up our signing."

They talked at length about how best to handle JK and then she said, "Going to go change now."

He looked at his watch. 12:20. "Why don't you wait until he calls? Airport's twenty minutes away." He smiled for the first time since their dance. "Besides, I love that dress. Want to enjoy it as long as possible. It'll be cooler by time he lands. Decide then what's best to wear. I suggest jeans."

His smile could convince her of anything. "Okay." She was feeling better but not all better. She was excited, so she didn't hear the inner murmur saying something wasn't quite right.

As they chatted, he said, "Remember, I've arranged a little R&R for tomorrow."

"Oh yeah."

"We can use it. And after tonight, we'll need it."

"Sounds good."

"Yep. Just you and me." He grinned. "The boat will be ready. We're going sailing"

"Yahoo."

He stood up and spread his arms.

She came around the table and walked into his embrace. It felt oh so good. *I need this.*

He stepped back. "Anchors up at six."

"What'll I wear? I didn't bring anything for sailing."

"All taken care of. Had the guys at the marina pick out your complete sailing wardrobe. Hat, shoes, shorts, tops. And you brought a sin-inspiring bikini, right?"

Her heart did a cartwheel.

Just after 1:00 am, he called JK and asked him their ETA. "Call when you're on the ground and I'll give you instructions to where we're meeting." He hung up and touched her arm. "Game time." His eyes were full of anticipation. "Go change."

She jumped up, put her hands in the middle of his massive chest, took his mouth lightly with a kiss that was full of want, excitement, love – and trust. "Back in five minutes."

CHAPTER ELEVEN

At first she thought the worst. Something bad had happened. She knocked and knocked on his door. Nothing. Maybe she misunderstood and he was waiting in the lobby. Not there. She went to the night manager at the front desk. "Excuse me. I'm looking for Mr. Walters. Has he been down in the last five minutes?"

"Is that the gentleman in the Grand Anse suite?" asked the young man.

"Yes, yes."

"I just came on duty. Let me see if Allister is still here." He disappeared into a back room and was back in a few seconds. "He says Mister Walters left about five minutes ago."

"Let me talk to him."

"Yes Ma'am."

The man called Allister looked frightened. "Help you Ma'am?"

"Are you sure you saw Mr. Walters? Leaving?"

"Yes Ma'am."

"You're certain?"

"Yes Ma'am."

"Did he say anything?"

"No Ma'am."

"Was anyone with him?"

"No Ma'am?"

"You're sure?"

"Yes Ma'am."

She didn't know if her nervousness or the clerk's repetitiveness was stoking her anger. Or the reality? "Did he take a cab?"

"No Ma'am."

Now she was pissed. "So how the hell *did* he leave?"

"In a limo, Ma'am."

She wanted to keep asking questions in hopes of getting a different answer. But she knew the truth. He'd played her. The anger and hurt spewed out. She half yelled at the clerk. "Thanks a lot."

"Yes Ma'am."

"I'm sorry. I didn't me to bark. I'm just ..."

"Yes Ma'am.

She turned and walked across the lobby and dropped into one of the large, wicker sofas. This was not good. Her emotions flashed like a hundred short-circuiting lightbulbs. Anger. Hurt. Disappointment. Hurt. Hurt. Hurt. The voice in her head just kept repeating, *How? How? How? ... How could he?* After the ache subsided a little, the question became, *Why would he?*

It must have been thirty minutes before she noticed the night manager staring at her, probably wondering what the hell she was doing hanging out in the lobby at 2 am. She had no idea. Other than she had no energy or interest in getting up and going to her room. At least here she wasn't completely alone, there was the night manager. She admonished herself and started to plan what she was going to do, must do, when he showed up. If he did. Her biggest worry was for his safety, but it was drowned out by the mad voice in her head. *How dare he? How could he? Why would he?* She focused on the last question.

In the cool night air with the sound of the surf in the distance, she began to go over what was happening. She heard the voice of her dad, *first the necessary, then the useful, then the pleasant.* Yale's safety was necessary. Protecting Apogee was necessary. Uncovering his secret was necessary. Avoiding irrational arguments with him was useful, but not necessary. And the pleasant could wait. Obviously, they wouldn't be having some romantic sail in the morning. That sure as hell wasn't necessary. Or useful under the circumstances.

She cautioned herself to remain calm when he returned. Whenever that would be?

• • •

"Victoria...." He gently touched her shoulder. She was all scrunched up, like a kitten, except for her long, lissome legs, in form-fighting jeans, dangling off the side of the wicker sofa. "Victoria ..."

"What ...? Oh ... sorry." She sat up awkwardly.

He so wanted to pick her up and carry her back to his room and just tuck her into bed. But he knew what was coming.

Just the sight of him made her feel better. Still groggy, she sputtered, "Thank god you're okay." Then everything came back to her. She started with, "Where the hell have you been?" And then she fired off all the questions she'd been asking herself. He just sat next to her and listened.

When she stopped, he took her hands. "You may never forgive me. I realize that. I understand. I understand trust is everything ... and I may have broken that bond with you. Because – "

She sat up straighter. "What do you mean 'may have?' You did." She heard the edge in her voice as it echoed across the empty lobby. She saw the night manager staring at them. "Let's discuss this in our room."

At least she still calls it our room.

Back in the room, she had no idea what she was going to say. So she avoided. "I need coffee. A lot." She went to the kitchenette and hoped he'd know where to start. The coffeemaker wasn't working either. "Shit." She hit it. "Fuck."

"Here, let me." He avoided brushing against her but when he looked in her eyes he saw that beyond the exhaustion was hope.

She wanted him to help. She didn't want to fight. "I need it strong. And black."

"You got it Beautiful."

He fixed it. *He was so damn good at everything – everything but trust.*

"There … It'll take a few minutes. Let's sit." He went to the table, she followed. "I'd like to take a few minutes and explain myself and then give you as much time as you want." He leaned closer but didn't touch her. "I met with JK. Wasn't pretty. Ferocious argument. Just the two of us. His driver was a couple hundred feet away. Mine too. We went at it for about an hour, I guess. Although there was no agreement, I think I got what I – we – need." As tired as she was, she was totally engaged. At one point he said, "There's part of this that I do not want to tell you – just yet. I will. Just not yet."

She rolled her eyes. "Here we go again. That trust me shit."

Victoria, no … Sorry, I understand how you feel. But I'll tell you on the boat today when – "

"That's a helluva assumption."

"Here me out." He reached across and put his hand on hers. It penetrated the unpleasantness. The sight of their hands together, his rugged strength on top, holding her securely. *I'll listen to him as long as he wants.* Then she slowly pulled her hand out from under his. *Why'd I do that?* Was it the need for independence? Or hurt by his deception? The glass table was cold.

He was calm and comforting even though the story was tense and frightening. The timbre of his voice soothed her. Part of her just wanted to curl up in his lap and listen, the other part wanted to kick his ass around the room.

He said. "When I showed him the photos the PI took of the two men entering his house, I thought he was going to explode." He didn't say, … *or pull a gun.* "I've seen him in the past when a deal has gone south but I've never seen him like this. Usually, he just stares. Fuming inside, cold on the outside. Not here. He stomped, kicked gravel on my shoes and called me the nastiest names. He didn't stop until he ran out of expletives."

She saw a slight grin, just a wrinkle at the corner of his mouth, as he tried to inject some levity.

"I guess losing a few hundred-million can do that?" His mouth tightened, and his beautiful teeth disappeared behind pressed lips. "Then he told me what was going to happen."

What Yale told her seemed filtered, not dishonest, just measured. JK had basically admitted he'd been compromised. That the photos of the Somalian and his lawyer at his New Jersey home and the State Department's awareness of his past arms dealing could mean the FBI would be on his trail soon. He knew he couldn't go through with the deal as long a Yale wanted to acquire the company. But he issued an ominous threat. Yale said. "He stuck a finger in my face and said, 'If you and that smart-ass, hot-shot, investment woman think this is over, think again. Your problems have just begun.'"

Victoria knew that wasn't verbatim, he'd cleaned up the language. And probably the ferocity. Maybe the threat? She stood up and walked to ease the uneasiness. Suddenly, "Oh my god!"

He stood up.

She was staring at the salt-water aquarium. "Is she dead? … she's dead."

"Who's dead?"

"Zofia … the octopus."

The octopus was floating on the surface. He walked over. "I am afraid so."

She sat down not knowing why she felt bad. *It's just an octopus – was. Probably died of old age.* "What could have happened?"

"I'll get rid of him. Some octopuses only live six months. It's criminal to keep them in captivity. Cruel."

She almost corrected him … *her.*

He disposed of the remains and returned to the table. He wanted to get back to the story. "JK ranted about burying Apogee and Kennor Capital in lawsuits and – "

"Do you think it means anything?" She was looking at the aquarium. "Like a premonition or something … Not that I believe in that crap but – ”

"Means nothing." He took her hand.

"Should you text her. Just check?"

"Who?"

"I nick-named the damn thing Zofia … in one of my jealous moments."

He waved a dismissive hand. "Nah. Don't let it bother you. The death of an octopus is not my concern. You're my only concern."

"And the deal. And JK."

"JK went on about suing Apogee and Kennor, disowning his daughter, getting us out of the way, and getting his multi-million-dollar pound of flesh, one way or the other. And he said, 'You know who's flesh it will be. Accidents do happen.'"

"Then it was my turn. I told him what was going to happen. I told him not to come within five miles of the Pentagon people and to be off the island before the sun came up. Or I'd be on the phone to State and FBI before his jet was in the air. He slinked away. He's gone … high over Barbados by now." He squeezed. "That's why I couldn't let you come with me. This man is irrational and unpredictable. You there would have made him worse. He hates women. No respect for them. He would've been relentless in berating you and I wouldn't have allowed it. I would've hit him. More than once. And that would have been disastrous. You see, I was the weak link. If I'd allowed you to be face-to-face, it would have unleashed my bad side. If he'd threatened you, I'd have killed him. Which would have sunk the deal, for sure."

My hero, protecting me. And then she thought of the dead octopus. She knew it was nothing, but couldn't shake the idea that its death meant something. She had two phobias, which she never admitted. Spiders and snakes. And that octopus was just as creepy – all those tentacles, slinking around. Now it was dead.

• • •

Her heart felt better by the time the sliver of dawn poked through the windows and her third cup of coffee had gone cold. Surprisingly, she had more energy than expected and although she wasn't up for running a marathon, she could sure do with some sunbathing on a sailboat. Especially one skippered by the handsome hunk sitting in front of her.

He said. "We've got less than an hour to get to the marina. I'm going to call Bernie. You want to call Kennor? Or is it too early?"

"No … I mean no, it's not too early. Probably up following European markets."

"Morning Carl. Hope it's not too early?" She summoned her steely business character. "Want to bring you up to date." She gave him an abbreviated version but carefully explained her financial strategy for protecting their investment. She finished with, "So with Kondracki out of the picture, I think we're in good shape."

After a long pause, Carl spoke. "Here's my concern. Your safety." Another long pause. "A few hundred-million will make a lot of men do crazy things. And someone like Kondracki … do even worse. We can handle the legal. But an irrational arms dealer, snarled in a deal with Somalians, that's a whole different game. I think you should get out of there. Today. Both of you."

Now she paused. He was frightening her. He never put personal before business. So if he was, it was serious. "Okay. I'll discuss it with Yale."

"I'm telling you, today."

"I hear you … Talk soon." She hung up.

"What was that?"

"He's up to date. Okay with it." She was hovering between Carl's advice and being alone on a sailboat with this once-in-a-lifetime man. She had so much emotional disruption to make up for. Today, not tomorrow.

He pushed. "What were you going to discuss with me?"

"Oh … just … whether he should contact State again or not.

Which as you said, doesn't have to happen with JK on his way back to New York."

He noticed she didn't make eye contact. Wasn't like her. But there was no way he could question her avoidance or honesty. Not him, the king of mistrust. He'd talk about it on the boat, after he told her his final secret. He hated to. But feeling the way he did about her, he had to trust her. "Yeah, no need. Now let's get to the marina, the wild blue ocean awaits."

CHAPTER TWELVE

Dressed in shorts and a hoody over a T-shirt, he took her breath away as she walked behind him onto the pier. Knowing she'd soon be alone with him in a very isolated place, a kaleidoscope of shameless images tumbled through her mind. And he wouldn't be wearing those shorts and T-shirt. *Wonder who steers the boat when he's in all his glory underneath me?*

He stopped. Looked back at her and then nodded at the most stunning boat she'd ever seen.

"Oh my god … this is …?"

"All yours baby."

She'd seen boats owned by wealthy people and she'd seen this boat before, in a photo on the wall in his office. But standing next to it, it was so much more magnificent. She was speechless. The luxury. The shine. The wood. The stainless steel. It had a number on the side, 50.3, which she thought meant it was fifty feet long. But it seemed bigger. And she loved the name, *Deckadence*. Still staring she asked. "When did it get here?"

"Had her sailed down from Key Largo. Got here last night." He stepped aboard and held out a hand.

Then she said something that must have come from one of the hundreds of movies she'd watched. "Permission to come aboard, Captain?"

He grinned, looked around. Nobody within earshot. "Get your gorgeous, irresistible, perfect ass on this boat Ms. Dyson … now."

She stepped into her fantasy.

At the end of a quick tour, her blood rush made her giddy.

What he called the 'fore-cabin' was what she dreamed heaven might be like. A large wall-to-wall bed with windows onto the ocean – portholes on all sides and a hatch, open to the vast blue sky. She could be happy here, with him, for the rest of her life.

He left her sitting in the large cockpit while he directed two young men to stow some supplies. She noticed several bottles of his favorite Chardonnay, Kistler. It was the same one they'd shared on that unrequited evening in his office.

He said. "Be back in a jiff. Gotta get your clothes." She soaked it all in, allowing the early morning breeze, although slightly cool, tingle across her face, pulling her into the moment. There were no problems. No Kondracki. No Kennor. No money. Just him. And everything she'd ever dreamed of.

"Okay. Here you go." He handed her a bag with tops, shorts, sandals and boating shoes. "You can change below." When she came back up he simply stared. *Every boat I ever sail will be adorned by this woman.* "Hey, I didn't know you brought those Purdue shorts. Perfect."

She winked. "Slipped them in, in case you needed a reminder." She pointed at a couple of bulky raincoats he was holding. "What are those for?"

"All-weather gear. Sailors always plans for the worse." He flipped up the top of one of the long seats and threw them in.

She pouted. "It ain't gonna rain on our parade is it?"

"Never." He reached for her hand. "Okay first-mate, time to set sail. This is a working holiday, all crew on deck." He pointed to one of the two big wheels in the cockpit and said, "Grab the helm and once we're away, you can guide us into the bay."

What? This thing is too damn big for me to steer. He was up and down the boat like a jungle cat. The two young men just stood and watched. It was obvious he didn't need any help. He pressed a button and the engine rumbled to life. He jumped out, untied the lines and the boat began to drift away. She was enthralled by his athleticism, his muscles bulging and his skin beginning to glisten with sweat. Just as the gap between the pier and the boat widen enough to scare her, he jumped on board. "Hey Beautiful. You're in charge. Pay attention."

"Yikes. Can I do this?"

"Sure. I'll man the throttle. Just ease her between those two pillions, point her out and head for the open sea."

One of the young men shouted out. "Have a great sail. Keep an eye on the weather."

He said. "Roger that." His smile was as big as the ocean and for a moment she damn near forgot what she was doing.

"If in doubt, keep that hill with the fort on top to your starboard." He crossed behind her and patted the right side of her butt. "Starboard is your right side, first-mate."

He was busy pulling lines, tightening things and then he opened the throttle a little more. She let the quickening breeze wash over her. She had never – never – been happier.

He sat for a moment on the edge of the cockpit and took her in. All of her. Every inch. She was so sexy, right down to her bare feet and French pedicure. And those never-ending legs that disappeared into the sexiest shorts he'd ever seen, which accentuated the beauty of her bare tummy, which wasn't just flat, it was concave, rising to the skimpiest halter top he could buy. And her thick, blonde hair, tight to her head, framed the inimitable joy in her face. Two loves, one place. Victoria. And sailing. A dream unfolding before his eyes. "Let's set those sails mate. Stop looking so beautiful and press the red off-button."

As the engine went quiet, she felt the thrust of the wind as the sails unfurled and the boat leapt forward, like a tiger unleashed. The speed hit seven knots, then eight. The exhilaration was consuming. He'd taken the other helm and it was all she could do not to jump on him and shout for joy. His brawn had always sent ripples of urgency through her but here, in the rising sun and stiffening breeze, his height and thickness pictured against the waves was what she imagined Ulysses and legendary seafarers must have looked like. Straining body, intense mind, surging muscles, all running against sea. She could not escape the seductive forces, strengthening like the wind, willing her toward freedom.

As the initial elation subsided, she realized the problem, their problem. Sailing was constant work. In a wind that he said was 15 to 20 knots, there wasn't much time for prolonged romantic forays and certainly none for love-making. She didn't know how long she could keep gawking at this man and not ravage him. And every time he let her take the helm, he would trim the sails, touch her, kiss her. Then loosen a line, touch her, kiss her. She was glowing, and her inner need was over-heating. But she couldn't let go of the wheel, she had no idea what would happen to the boat. *Would it tip over?*

Then he changed everything. He came and stood behind her, close. It was cramped quarters. He put his arms around her and hands on top of hers resting on the wheel. She tightened her grip.

He whispered above the wind. "She's on course. Close hauled and making good headway. She reminds me of you. Spectacularly beautiful. Great lines, perfect form, head strong and sexy, sexy, sexy." He pressed against her.

She drew in a large breath of salty air as his erection nestled between the round of her cheeks.

"As my first-mate, do you think you can skipper Deckadence for a little longer? With a steady hand?"

"I can't promise anything. Especially a steady hand … But I could give you a hand." She pulled her right hand out from under his and dropped it to her side.

"Be careful. You should hold on with two hands in case a rogue wave hits or – "

"You're the only rogue. And if you keep holding me this tight,

I won't need two hands." She reached behind her and took his hardness in her hand. "Now I'm holding on."

"Tighter."

She squeezed.

He pressed. And dropped a hand from the wheel. "We have to keep two hands on the wheel at all times – one of yours, one of mine."

She whispered feebly, "Okay." And then squeezed him again.

He pressed his hand into her heat. She was powerless, trapped between the force of his hand and the hardness of his desire. She pulled at his shorts. He yanked her Purdue shorts down. She was not sure what happened between that moment and the moment he was hard, up inside her. She clung to the wheel. His fingers pressed into her folds as his groans raced off with the wind. He moved in rhythm with the boat as it pushed into the endless waves, mounting and crashing like a pounding heart, as he slammed into her uncontrollable waves. The boat rose, rocked and heaved as her inner crescendo screamed for release. His demanding fingers stroked her, hard and fast, and she exploded, cries of joy sweeping across the ocean as his heat roared through her like the thundering sea. She lost all awareness, but felt everything.

They slumped to the seat, immobilized. He hung onto the wheel with one hand as he cradled her spent body in his lap.

With a dirty, little chuckle he said, "My plan was to get to Dragon Bay, where I'd make wild passionate love to you."

She turned and kissed his forehead. "Captain, your wish is my command. But I could not have waited. Not another minute."

"Well, it'll take a little longer now, we're off course."

She kissed him again. "Anything I can do?"

"Yeah. Stay on course while having intercourse with me."

Their laughter danced with the waves.

Later, she was sun bathing on the foredeck in her yellow bikini bottom when he yelled out. "I was thinking. Since there's no urgent need to anchor in Dragon Bay for love-making, what say we head north for a real sail? And then you won't have to put your top on. That's my selfish reason."

"Aye, aye Captain." She sat up on her towel and sent him that enchanting smile. "You've already proven you can handle this ship, this woman and this ocean, all at the same time." She stood up, slipped her bikini bottom off and tossed it in his direction. It blew overboard. "Oh, oh … now we can never return to land."

In all her naked splendor she came back to the cockpit. "Teach me how to sail Captain. And by the way, I've already learned why they call this place the cockpit?"

He patted her bare bottom. "Stand by to come about."

"Again?"

"No, no … not you, the boat. Means changing course."

"Again? More intercourse."

"Stop it. We've got work to do."

"At your command Captain."

He grinned. "Go below and get some clothes on so the Captain can concentrate. I've sailed the Seven Seas, but you're putting us at great risk wandering around like that.

"Aye, aye Captain." She turned and climbed down the companionway.

It was thirty-five nautical miles to the island of Carriacou, too far to go in a day, but he could head north-northwest for a couple of hours. Once they got beyond the lee of Grenada, the sea would be running at five to six feet. Fun. There'd been some weather in the forecast, but the high clouds suggested they'd be good for several hours, maybe the rest of the day. He'd have them back in St. George's by sundown.

As Deckadence cut through the water in a brisk 20 knot breeze, he showed her all kinds of things about the boat and what she could do to help. It was pure joy. As they sailed away from land the waves got bigger and the boat heeled over, putting the rail in the water.

She didn't know much about sailing, but with these winds it didn't look like they'd be indulging in love-making for a while. She was practicing trimming the foresail when she noticed he was gazing off into the distance. She watched him. Alert. Intense.

"Wow! Son of a bitch." He looked at her. "Stand by to come about."

"What?"

"Just sit low in the cockpit and when I say so, grab that winch handle and start grinding. And keep your head down."

He'd just taught her this stuff so she knew what to do. But not why. She recognized he was in go mode so no time for questions. Quickly, he spun the wheel, the boat lurched, the big boom swung across, the boat shuddered.

"Crank it in," he shouted.

The boat jumped forward.

After the flurry of action, she looked up and he was beaming, standing on the aft-deck, one hand on the wheel. "Ms. Dyson, you are in for the thrill of a lifetime."

"Already had the thrill of my lifetime," she shouted above the wind.

He pointed off the starboard side. "There, north, northeast. A mile out."

She stood up, hanging onto the rail. Saw nothing. "What?"

"Just watch for what looks like a puff of smoke … There!"

"I don't see anything."

"Watch."

"For what?"

"For the biggest thrill you've ever had."

"You're the biggest thrill I've ever had."

"This is bigger."

"Impossible."

"Just wait."

He stood on the high side, gazing over the sea. She looked

again. Then there was a kind of puff of smoke. "I saw it, I saw it ... the puff ... what is it?

"A blow ... humpback whales. A pod."

"Oh my god ... are we safe?"

At that moment, a whale breached, soaring out of the water.

"Yahooo.... Did you see that?"

"I did, I did. Incredible."

He turned the boat more in their direction.

"How close are we going?" She couldn't decipher between her excitement and fear.

He was all excitement. "Right smack in the middle of them."

He dropped the self-furling mainsail and trimmed the foresail, slowing the boat. In no time, he yelled, "Victoria look, look ... there."

About a hundred feet off the starboard side, gliding alongside the boat, was a giant whale. It was as long as the boat. She could see its eyes. "I think she – he – is looking at me. Oh my god ... oh my god."

He beamed. "Say it again. It may be as close to god as you ever get. He loved her excitement. She was jumping up and down like she was back at Purdue cheerleading. "Hang on. Don't fall in." He would have gone up and jumped with her – *jumped all over her* – but he needed to maneuver carefully among these beautiful beasts. He'd seen humpbacks before, been alongside, but only with one or two. Here there must have been a dozen, or more. There were several young ones and it had been one of the babies leaping over a cow when they were half-a-mile away. Now they were in their midst. He'd heard stories of how fishermen encountered pods like this so knew it was safe to be among them. But he didn't want to disturb them. Just mosey along and let them decide if they wanted to play.

She had gone below to get her camera and was draped over the railing taking photos. She felt as if she could reach out and touch this magnificent creature. It looked as if the whale was beckoning her, saying, 'hello, my new best friend.' Just then the water under the boat darkened … and before she could move, out of the water came a big, scary thunderous whale. She screamed and swallowed a gallon of salt water. The whale rose out of the water, soaring up and over her new best friend, landing with an enormous splash on the other side. She was drenched. Her scream turned to glee, happiness and tears.

He allowed the moment to sink in, saying nothing. He let it etch into his mind and heart. It was a lifetime memory. In that moment, love and life were one and the same. He loved this woman, who was leaning over the rail of his fifty-foot boat and getting drenched by a breaching twenty-foot calf, weighing two-or-three tons. She was soaking wet in her skimpy Purdue shorts and a wet T-shirt, looking at him as if to say, 'what the hell just happened?' She'd never looked happier, more excited, more beautiful. He laughed. "Ms. Dyson, you have just been baptized into a very special corner of the world." As she came to him he saw her tears.

She wanted to run to him but had to hold the railing and walk carefully. She was overwhelmed with joy and as she licked the salt from her lips the tears flowed. He spread one, big strong arm out and she rolled into it. He wrapped her in the embracing warmth of his body.

Neither said anything. She remembered how big the boat had seemed when she first saw it but now it seemed like a toy alongside these giants of the deep.

He kissed the top of her head. "Don't ever forget this. Few have experienced it. I never have. I've seen whales but never this many, this close." He squeezed her. "And for the rest of my life, I will never be able to offer you a shower like that." He tilted her head back and kissed her. "I love you."

She wiped the tears away. "I love you."

CHAPTER THIRTEEN

The whales had continued southward and for the last hour they'd been enjoying an invigorating sail, heading northwest. The exhilaration had slowly drifted, like a dream, off into the Caribbean breeze as she sat quietly, absorbing the reality. He told her that her new best friend was almost as long as the boat, probably forty-feet plus, and the baby that jumped weighed more than a couple of cars.

She was sitting on the high side of the cockpit, braced with her feet and taking in the panorama as he carved the boat through the water. The waves were bigger now and every so often he'd shout, 'hold on,' and a wave would crash over the bow and rush through the cockpit and out the back. It was breathtaking. She didn't want to admit it, but it was a little nerve-wracking too. She wasn't afraid – at least she kept telling herself that – but they sure looked like a tiny cork bobbing around on a tumbling ocean. Her comfort was in her man. Watching him work not only stirred longings but calmed her fears. No matter how many times they'd made love, seeing his physical strength in action triggered visceral lust. But with the boat racing along at nine knots, she knew her fantasies would have to wait until they were back on dry land.

He calculated they were more than twenty nautical miles from Carriacou and would soon have to head back. But he loved this sailing, it was electrifying … and with Victoria on board it was the ultimate ride. The wind and waves were picking up, waves seven to eight feet, wind out of the northeast at 25 knots. *Deckadence* handled it with ease.

She sensed it before she saw it. He was more intense. Watching the sky, scanning the horizon. Before he'd been talking to her, smiling, soaking up the adventure, but now he was less focused on her.

He shouted out. "Stand by to come about. Just crank that winch when I say so. And keep your beautiful head down. That boom will swing across fast. Ready …? Hang on."

"Ready." She knew what to do.

"Coming about."

The boat turned into an oncoming wave that thundered over the bow and roared over her feet. The boat slowed, leveled off and for a moment sat like a bull facing its foe, before charging. The sound of the sails wildly flapping in the wind was almost deafening. The boom swung across and then caught the wind, dove into the running waves and headed south-southeast. She was going home.

"You okay Hon?"

She wasn't sure. "I'm good … I'm good."

He motioned to her. "Come here. But hang onto something – always." He put his arm around her tiny waist. *Geez, she is so beautiful and fragile … and shaking.* "The ride should be easier now. Less pounding. We're running with the waves. There'll be times you'll look astern and think the wave is coming right in over us. But it won't. It lifts the boat and runs underneath." He smiled and squeezed her tighter. He looked back. "Here comes one now. Watch."

She turned, clinging to him even tighter. A half-scream slipped out. "… Yale!"

"It's okay."

The wave seemed like it was twenty feet above them. And then the back of the boat rose like an elevator and slid down the wave like a rollercoaster.

"Shit. That's scary."

He kissed the top of her head. "No problem." He patted the console. "This baby can handle anything." He relaxed his hold on her. "I want you to do something. As a precaution. Under that seat, in that locker are lifejackets. I want you to put one on and get one for me."

"Okay." She heard her own fear.

"It's just a precaution. The seas have picked up and all sailors, even the best, wear lifejackets when necessary. And always hang onto to something when navigating the deck."

She felt better after she put the lifejacket on and saw him in his. "Don't you have this in pink?" She smiled. "Goes better with my outfit." She noticed he laughed but was more intent on the sky behind them. Amid all the excitement she hadn't noticed the clouds darkening in the sky.

She sat back and decided to enjoy the ride, it was like a monster rollercoaster. She could see why he loved sailing. One-on-one, man against the sea. Powerful and yet humbling. In charge of your destiny but at war with nature. It was a constant struggle, boat and man – and woman – and the endless sea. It was, for her, a personal high, a once in a lifetime adventure, a walk on the wild side, a million miles away from the glass-ceiling world she lived in. She watched him watching the wind and waves and sky. He was in his element. Her Ahab. She chuckled, *and we've already met Moby Dick.*

After thirty minutes the clouds had thickened, the wind strengthened, and the waves grown. She'd put on a jacket he'd brought, it was yellow not pink, and he'd laughingly said, 'It matches your lost bikini.' She was warmer now, but it didn't take care of the growing fear. She kept her gaze on the far horizon, eager to see the sight of land. At one point, he went below and turned on the radio, which was now reporting static-filled weather messages. He told her that once they were in the lee of Grenada, the weather would ease. She hoped it was soon.

He shouted above the wind. "Victoria, in that same locker,

under the seat, you'll find two blue safety harnesses. Get them out … just precaution." As he watched her fumbling in the locker his safety concerns increased. She was his ultimate responsibility. The clouds were now very high and forming thunderheads. He shouted. "Also, there's a couple clips and lines – rope – in a pouch hanging on the side of the locker. Bring'em too." As she maneuvered across the few feet of wet deck toward him, he knew his entire future was standing – actually, stumbling – right in front of him. She looked like a beautiful, frightened, wet lioness. Proud. Standing tall. But wary. He took her hand. "Hold onto this bar." He took the gear from her. "We're gonna be fine. Trust me." They laughed.

"I trust you." She coughed.

"This stuff is precautionary." He slipped the safety harness over her and clipped a line to the front of it and to the railing. He did the same. "Just sit there and relax." It was now a race against time. "I'm gonna get every ounce outta this girl."

"I'll bet you say that to all the girls." He didn't answer, he was in go mode.

He released the sails a little more and leaned into the helm, becoming one with the boat. At some point, he locked the wheel, tethered his harness and went to the companion way. "Be right back." He popped up with a radio in his hand. "Grenada, this is Deckadence, Grenada, this is Deckadence … Over." He waited.

"Deckadence, this is Grenada … Over."

"We're five nautical miles north-northwest of Ronde Island. Weather deteriorating. What's report out of Carriacou? … Over."

"Latest. Gale force seven … repeat gale force seven … over."

He looked a stern. "Grenada, thanks … Over."

"Deckadence … wait. Had someone ask for you … Over."

"Ask for me? … Over"

"Roger that. Three men … Over."

She clenched the grab-bar.

"What did they want? … Over."

"Asked where you'd gone. When? … Said were friends." Chartered a powerboat. Think went looking for you."

"What names did they log? … Over."

"Let me look … yeah. One guy signed. Looks like Kond … Kond-something-or-other. Initials JK … Over."

Her fear froze somewhere between her cold, bare legs and her heart.

"Grenada, this is important … Need to know exactly when departed. Size and type of boat … over."

"Roger that. Give me a sec …" He was back. "Departure 2:40. Chartered a 514PC catamaran. It's a beauty. Biggest we got … Over."

"Roger that. What kind of headway does she make? … Over."

"Twin 350s … maybe 12-13 knots … Over."

"Roger that … over and out."

"My god … he's coming after us," she said.

He reached over and pulled her close but said nothing. He scanned the sails above, the sky behind, the horizon beyond. As frightened as she was, she felt an inner comfort with him. And there was no place she'd rather be. Except on land.

He could see heavy rain approaching from the north. His first choice was to make land at the north end of Grenada. Or Ronde Island which was closer but not as sheltered, and a real bastard to navigate in heavy seas. His last option was Carriacou – back into the storm. His main worry was Victoria. He knew the boat could handle it. And he could. He'd sailed in many storms but with experienced sailors. And these seas were running high and gale force seven could turn into nine in a blink. He pulled her closer.

"What are we going to do?" Not wanting to sound frightened or too dependent, she asked, "What can I do?"

He kissed her wet, salty hair. "Keep your safety line clipped at all times. When I tell you, I want you to go and sit by the other wheel and hold on to the grab bar. If I need you to do anything, I'll yell. If not, don't panic." He tugged her waist. "This boat won't sink, ever. Remember that. We'll take on a lot water, but it won't capsize." He looked deep into her eyes, "Okay?" He thought about telling her that if it did go over, it would right itself, but saw no reason to put such an idea in her head.

"Okay." The wind was so loud she wasn't sure he heard. His eyes were like steel, face like granite. He looked like a prizefighter stepping into the ring. She repeated as confidently as she could, "Okay. But there must be something I can do?" She wasn't about to sit there like a frightened cat.

"Go sit at the other helm. And give me the readings. Compass direction. Speed. About every minute." He didn't really need it, but it was good to keep her involved. "I'm going to reef the main and may need you. Stand by mate."

She liked the sound of that even though she wished she'd had a little more practice being his mate. She held the bar and never took her gaze off the console. The boat was now running down each wave like a huge avalanche and she didn't dare look back at the waves just before they roared underneath this tiny, shuddering boat that he assured her, *wouldn't sink.* She completely trusted him. Completely.

He was talking – more yelling. It was a good way to keep her involved and not overly focused on the elements. He checked the weather astern. Peered south to the horizon. Visibility was deteriorating. "We should be about two miles north, northwest of Ronde."

She shouted. "South, southeast, 120 degrees. 9.8 knots." Between readings she looked over at him. He was bigger than any Ahab. Stronger. Tougher. And drop-dead gorgeous. *Oh, no. Why did I pick that word?*

"Tell me when the compass reads 110?" He hoped to get to Ronde Island before JK spotted them. And he'd love to be at anchor when the storm peaked. As for JK, catamaran cruisers were notoriously unstable in heavy weather and if this storm gets to gale force nine, they're in trouble. Hopefully they don't head for shelter at the same island.

She yelled. "110 … 9.9 knots."

He glanced at her. Wet and afraid, she was the only thing in the world that mattered. He would get them through this. Because the weather was behind them, he could still see about half-a-mile to the south and he thought for a second he saw land. Ronde Island had a couple of high hills and the anchorage he needed was around the headland at the north corner. But there were two jutting rocks called 'The Sisters' that had to be navigated. It wouldn't be a walk in the park.

It was time to reef the mainsail. He did not want to give up speed, but the wind was increasing. He hit the self-furling to bring it down. Nothing. He tried again. Nothing. Not wanting to head into the wind, he let the main out more to spill wind. But he still had to get it down. The boom was too close to the water. If a big wave swamped the main they'd go over. And she was not strong enough to winch it. "Victoria. I want you to do something. I'm going to give you the wheel. That one." He pointed at the big wheel in front of her. "When I say go, just grab the wheel and hold the boat steady on 110. Every wave will push you off a little but just bring it back. Okay?"

She felt like a deer in the headlights. "Okay." She stood up, both hands clenching the wheel.

"Ready … go!" With brute strength, he winched the boom in as much as possible and then jumped up on the deck, grabbed the mast and climbed up on the boom.

She watched in horror. My god, he could fall into the ocean and be gone. Her heart dropped out of her body. She forced herself to look at the compass, away from him dangling from the mast. When she glanced up, he had a big knife in his hand. *What the hell is that for*? Suddenly, he cut a long slit in the sail. And then another, and another. And as he did, he inched out on the boom. She thought she was going to gag from holding her breath. Her life was hanging in the balance on that boom.

He yelled down at her. "Lock the wheel ... lock it. Do it."

She did.

"Okay, now winch the mainsail more. As much as you can."

She jumped across the cockpit and started winching as hard as she could. It moved. She strained until her muscles shrieked.

He yelled. "Okay. Back to the helm. Unlock it and get on course." He reached out and made several more cuts and then dropped to the deck and back in the cockpit. "Great job mate. Got it now."

She sat. Frightened. Exhausted. For a moment, the noise was a distant hum. She was unaware of anything except her heart. *I could've lost him.*

He was yelling into the wind. "Fuckin' roller jammed. Wouldn't come down. Had no choice."

Through sheets of hardening rain, she could now see an island in the distance. "How far is that?"

He was too busy to answer. It was Ronde, but they were maybe a mile off with a wicked squall bearing down on them, it would hit in a few minutes. They couldn't make it. He made a decision. "Victoria. Listen carefully. I'll talk you through this." He reached across and squeezed her hand. With a reassuring grin he said, "You can do this ... trust me."

She never wanted to let go of his hand.

"Unlock your wheel. You're going to stay this course, 110 until I tell you to come about. When I do, you're going to turn the wheel hard. I mean hard. As hard as you can. To port ... left. And you hold it hard until it's pointing into the wind. You can tell because the Ginny, that sail upfront will be flapping wildly. The compass will be about 340. It's important you hold it there. In the wind, sail flapping. Got it?

She nodded and repeated it. "Hard left. 340. Flapping in the wind."

"And we'll keep it there until I get that sail trimmed."

He was up and gone, racing along the rail to the bow of the

boat. She felt the dark fear rising in her gut, her chest, her throat. He was like a mountain lion. She had no idea what he was doing. Then he yelled.

"Now. Now. Hard. Hard. Hard."

She had no idea where her strength came from. She hammered that wheel around until it wouldn't go any further. She watched the compass. Nothing much seemed to be happening. *Did I not do it right?* Gradually the boat shifted. Like an overweight hippo, it moved. She saw the sail at the front start to flap and then suddenly it slammed past the middle and started out the other side. He was scrambling all over. He shouted. "Back. Back. Back a little." She wasn't sure what to do. She looked at the compass. It was at 330. *Oh shit.* She turned the wheel hard right. It moved. And the sail flapped again. He did a bunch of things and soon the sail was just a small triangular piece. He dropped into the cockpit and grabbed the wheel.

"Great job." He started the engine.

The sound of the engine made her jump, but she was glad to have him back next to her. She waited a few beats and then said. "Can I ask what we're doing?"

"Hang tight."

He was wrestling with the wheel, the boat, the waves, the wind. She left him alone.

He pushed the throttle full and the engine strained against what he now estimated were ten-foot waves, winds pushing 40-45 knots. He had both hands on the wheel and he pressed his body into hers. She locked her arm inside his.

He yelled in her ear. "We're too far off Ronde to make it before the squall hits. It would push us onto the reef. We're gonna take on the squall." He looked at her. "A piece of cake."

There was a small grin at the corner of his mouth. And no fear in his eyes. They were steady, intense, fierce. And reassuring. Despite the angry sea looking like it was ready to swallow them up in one monstrous wave. She tugged his arm. "Anything I can do?"

"Crouch low, hang onto the edge of the seat and crawl over to the locker and get a red double clip. And the extra line that's there. In that same pouch." He gripped her forearm and eased her away from him. "Ready?"

"Ready." It wasn't as hard as she thought. The boat seemed to be more level than before, and she was back in no time.

He said. "Take the wheel and hold her right here, straight into the wind." He took the clips and line from her, tied a clip to each end of the line and clipped one end on the ring on the front of her safety harness and the other end to the ring on his. He took the wheel. "Okay. We've now officially tied the knot." This time his grin was bigger.

For just a second, she saw only him, his wet, hard-edged jaw, burning eyes and the indomitable energy of his body. The roiling sea was just backdrop.

"Just a precaution…. This way I got you, no matter what." He turned back to the sea.

"So what's the plan Ahab?"

He looked straight ahead and calculated the squall, then explained. The idea was to head straight into it with only a tiny triangular piece of the foresail flying to give the boat stability. She thought she understood. She trusted him. When the storm hit, he wanted her to sit on the floor of the cockpit and hold onto the seat leg. He added, "And my leg." He would stay at the helm and power the boat through the waves. He said it would be loud and rough and torrential. And the waves would crash over the bow and through the cockpit with a lot of force but all she had to do was brace her feet and hang on. "You'll probably drink a few gallons of sea water but just keep spittin' it out." Then he took a hand off the wheel, wrapped his arm around her shoulders, hugged her hard.

She looked up. *If I'm as wet as he is, my hair must look like hell.*

He kissed her. It was double wet – a lot of ocean and a lot of him. Again, for a second, there was only him. Only them.

She could no longer see Ronde Island behind them and it was a sinking feeling that they'd been that close to land and were now going the opposite way, out into an ugly, ugly ocean. *I wonder how the whales are doing? … what a stupid thought.*

The line squall line bore down on them and he steeled himself. This would be tricky. The wind would jump to maybe 60-70 knots.

She had not hunkered down on the floor yet and for some reason she glanced to the south, maybe hoping to sight land. Or a rescue boat? *Oh my god!* There was a boat. She just tapped his arm and pointed.

He saw it. He knew it. It was a 512PC. It was JK.

He assessed the situation. Distance. Direction. Headway. The twin-hulled, boat was maybe a mile off the port beam. It was heading southeast, away from them, probably for Ronde. It was floundering badly as it ran broadside to the waves. Dangerous. And stupid. Headway was hard to tell because it kept disappearing below the waves. He shouted in her ear. "Grab the binoculars." He took them from her. "Take the helm … straight into the wind."

She was amazed at how he kept his balance without hanging onto anything. He braced himself, legs spread, knees pressed against the wheel peering through the binoculars.

"Looks like three men. Definitely JK. Don't think they've seen us. They're in too much trouble. And headed for more. Good luck with that." He handed her the binoculars, took the helm and pushed the throttle.

Every time they mounted a wave and crashed down the other side she thought the boat was coming apart. It hit the water like a pancake and shook uncontrollably. She peered back every few seconds looking for JK's boat and only saw it once when it bobbed above the waves. Suddenly she yelled. "Yale … Yale. I think they've changed direction."

He swung around. "Binoculars!" He braced himself

and watched.

It seemed like an eternity.

"Assholes ... They're heading out." He pushed the throttle, even though it was wide open. "Okay boys. You want it. Come get it ... idiots."

Now she was frightened – scared to death. Would it be the sea or JK who got them? "What should I do?"

"Hang on. That squall will get here before they do."

"But they can catch us, right? Their boat is faster than ours, right?"

"Bigger, faster and a tub of danger." He glanced back. "Good chance that tub won't make it. Squall will eat it up and spit it out like a cork."

"Really?"

"We might be calling 'mayday' – for them."

"Or not?" she said. He shot her a look that she couldn't quite tell if he agreed.

He looked back. Then up. Then back. He shouted. "Get down on the floor." He put his hand on her head and pushed her down.

She noticed he sat down and hunched over.

"I think they're shooting at us. Heard a ping off the mast. Or something. Not sure. Squall's too close. Can't man the helm and hold binoculars."

"I'll do it." She raised herself to her knees and put her elbows on the back deck. All she could see was frothing, roaring water. Then the boat bobbed up on top of a wave. Then it was gone. She trained the binoculars on the spot where it disappeared. There it was again. Then gone. "Shit." She waited. Several times they were there and then gone before she could see much. And then they rose into the lens and hung there. One, two, three men. My god! One of them had a big long gun ... and then they disappeared below the waves. "Yes, yes. He has a gun."

"Get down. Squall's about to hit."

The rain was like sleet. The noise deafening. The fear suffocating. She thought the water roaring through the cockpit was going to sweep her overboard. She wrapped her arms around the table leg and her hands gripped his leg until her knuckles were white. Each time there was a pause between the torrents of water, she rubbed the stinging salt from her face and peeked up at him. He looked like a towering cliff on the edge of the sea, facing everything the storm threw at him, and taking it. At least she hoped he could. *I wonder if dad would think this was part of 'the necessary.' This is probably what happens when they put out those small craft warnings and the next day announce, 'couple lost at sea.'*

The squall was deeper, longer and nastier than he anticipated. The boat could handle it if he kept her hard into it. The radio crackled with static but even with the tumultuous sound of the storm he heard the mayday call.

CHAPTER FOURTEEN

"Mayday, mayday, mayday ... this is Quiet Waters ... come in ..." Static interrupted for what seemed like an eternity. It was a sailor's worst nightmare. A mayday.

He knew there was nothing he could do. His sole responsibility was to make sure he didn't have to make a similar call.

"Mayday, mayday, mayday ... north, northwest ..." More static. "Ronde island ... Static. Then nothing.

Deckadence took everything the sea served up that day and they soon emerged on the other side of the squall. Winds dropped to 35-40 knots and it was the proverbial calm after the storm. He'd held Victoria close and although she probably swallowed half the water that came onboard, she'd been safe – tethered to him. He reached down and touched her head. "Worst is over." He looked astern. "Or not?"

She wasn't sure she could get up.

He headed the boat north-northwest and ran the engine at full throttle.

In a few minutes, the radio cracked to life. "Deckadence come in, Deckadence come in ... This is Grenada ... Over."

He touched her. "Can you get that Hon. I'm going to unclip our tether. Just hold on as you go."

She looked like a new born foal as she wobbled across to the companion way and grabbed the radio.

He said. "Just say, Grenada, this is Deckadence ... Over."

The reply was troubling. "Deckadence. We had a mayday, north, northwest of Ronde. Where are you? ... Over."

He told her what to say. "Two nautical miles north, northwest of Ronde, heading 320 ... Over."

"Last report was in your area. Then lost contact. What's weather? ... Over."

They had a back and forth conversation with the coast guard that left him in a predicament. The coast guard confirmed that the boat, Quiet Waters, was a 512PC cruiser. He knew it was JK. He also knew that as the only boat in the vicinity of the mayday it was his responsibility to search for the boat and survivors.

"Deckadence, come in ... Over."

"This is Deckadence ... Over."

"We suspect last contact was south, southeast of your location, within a nautical mile or so. Are seas down? Can you to proceed with initial search? ... Over."

He gazed at the rolling sea, "Roger that ... Over."

"Coast guard boat out of Dragon Bay heading for your location. Be thirty minutes ... Over"

"Roger that. Will begin search ... Over."

"Roger ... Over and out."

In that moment, regardless of her fear, she could not have respected – or loved – him more. Her stoic sailor standing at the helm, peering into the gray unknown in complete control of an uncontrollable situation, and doing what was right. It would have brought her to tears of joy, except it was frightening to think what –

"Stand by to come about," he shouted.

They brought the boat to a south, southeast course and he had her take the helm. "Keep the engine running," he shouted from the foredeck. He dug all kinds of equipment and lines and life jackets out of the lockers and then came and put his arm around her shoulders. "This will be okay." He kissed her soaking hair. "Trust me." They both chuckled. What was ahead was completely unpredictable, perhaps more dangerous than what they'd just come through. As they plunged down the waves, he stood high on the seat scanning.

He'd given her a flare gun with instructions to hold it high and away from her body and fire it into the sky when he said. He also told her that if they found anyone in the water she would have to handle the wheel and he would give her instructions. He went over the rescue drill with her and said, "The chances of plucking someone from the water in these seas is next to impossible. But we have to try." He explained that at the very least, they would approach as close as possible and throw a trailing line and life ring out, so the person might grab it. And they would dump a life raft overboard for them. He said, "We'll stay in proximity until the coast guard arrives. Whether we find anyone … or two or three. Who knows?"

She was now cold and had a headache. *How could they see anyone in these waves?*

He stiffened. "Let me take the wheel." He moved next to her. "Just hang on."

She stared into the grayness. "There." She strained. "I saw something." She pointed starboard. "There – "

"I see him, I see him."

An orange lifejacket was bobbing like a tiny leaf on the black sea.

He started shouting instructions. "Keep your safety line fastened. Fire the flare straight up. Hold it as far away from you as you can. And turn your head away … then grab those two lifejackets … And the lifeline that's on the starboard cleat."

Adrenalin surged as she scrambled across the deck.

He knew the risk. Knew the odds. Rescuing someone from the ocean with a sailboat was tough at the best of times, let alone in a raging sea. First, he had to get close. But not too close. Then get a trailing line near enough that the person could grab it. That meant coming alongside and then coming about so that the line came to them. But not so close that risked the boat hitting them – probably drowning them. Or having the line rip across them before they could grab it. All this in seven-foot seas and thirty knot winds. He'd try one pass and if it was too dangerous or couldn't be done, he'd throw the life raft overboard and hope the person could get to it. Which was unlikely.

Everything was in slow motion. She kept staring at the bobbing life jacket, trying to see who it was. Finally, they were maybe a hundred feet away from a man who was alive. At one point, he waved, feebly. She'd never seen JK so didn't know who it was.

Yale shouted. "Stand by with lifejacket. Hold it until I say. But toss that line in the water, now."

Fear numbed her every step as she inched toward the rail, ready to throw the line and ring. She hurled it as hard as she could while hanging on for dear life.

"Good job," he shouted. "Now move forward with the lifejacket, to mid-ship if you can. And when I yell, throw it in JK's direction."

It is him. Thoughts tumbled. *Could they save him? What if they couldn't ... would anyone believe them?*

He maneuvered the boat within fifty feet of JK and then brought it around and up into the wind and waves. "Come here ... take the wheel. Hold it right here."

He grabbed the trailing line and yelled. "JK ... JK. Can you hear me?" He waved. "There's a line in the water with a life ring. Keep your hands out and feel for it. Grab it and hang on. You'll only have a few seconds."

He came back and took the wheel. He watched the line in the water and when it looked close to JK, he slowed the engine, slammed it into reverse and then pushed it to full throttle. The boat shuddered and seemed to stand still for a few seconds. Now! Now! ... Grab it!"

They both watched. A desperate man, a small life ring, a thin hundred-foot line and a raging sea.

"He got it. Quick take the wheel. Hold steady." He pushed the throttle and began to slowly pull JK toward the boat.

She took her eyes off the compass once to glance back. She saw the man dip below the surface, but he was still holding the life ring when he reappeared. It seemed to take forever, and her muscles were aching as she fought to hold the boat into the waves. Yale was everywhere. Up, back, down. Tying another line to a lifejacket and throwing it over the side and then tying a line to the ladder and putting it over the side. She just stared at the compass.

"Good…. Good…. I got the wheel now. Go to the ladder and help him aboard."

When she looked down she saw an exhausted, almost-dead, little man hanging on the bottom rung of the ladder. Instinctively she leaned over.

"Don't lean," yelled Yale. "Pull the rope. Don't take his hand. Only the line. He could pull you overboard. If he falls back in, let go of the line, immediately."

She took the slack out of the rope and pulled until the ring under his armpits looked as if it was going to come up over his head. "He's not trying. I'm afraid I might pull the ring off."

"He's taken in a lot of water. Just lightly tug the ring and see if he responds. Yell at him. Tell him he has to do it."

She began yelling, and tugging on the ring. Slowly he raised himself to the next rung, and the next. Then his head came up over the gunwale. He looked dead.

"Good job. Take the wheel. I'll get him onboard."

Yale threw JK's limp, saturated body into the cockpit like it was a hooked fish. He quickly fastened a line to his lifejacket, secured it and took the helm. He squeezed her arm. "We did it."

She smiled, even though she didn't think there was much to smile about. They were still somewhere in the middle of an angry ocean, no land in sight and an arms dealer who had been shooting at them now on board. She was cold and exhausted. She leaned into the wet warmth of his legs as he stood at the helm, immersed in the incessant battle with the sea. Between waves, he would wrap a reassuring arm around her shoulders and despite the fatigue, she felt okay – at least for the moment.

JK had revived a little and raised himself onto the seat. He was a diminutive man, *couldn't be more than a hundred-and-fifty-pounds soaking wet.* Pale and lifeless. Yale instructed her to pour several bottles of water over him to wash the salt off and get him a towel, blankets and bottled water to drink. He squeezed her hand, "Thank you."

"Deckadence, this is Coast Guard One … come in … over."

She grabbed the radio. "Coast Guard One … this is Deckadence … over."

"Saw your flare. What's your position? … over."

She looked at Yale and shrugged. Then repeated what he said. "North, northwest of Ronde. Estimate two nautical miles. Heading, south, southeast, 130. … over."

"Roger that. We have two men onboard. No sign of the third. Or the boat … over."

"Coast Guard One. We have a man onboard. Alive. A little worse for wear … over."

"Roger that. Good work Deckadence … over."

"Ditto, Coast Guard One…. What's weather and seas where you are? … over."

"Three nautical miles south, south west Ronde … heading for Dragon Bay. Sea running five-six, weather clearing … over."

"Coast Guard One. Have damaged sails … heading to Ronde. … over."

"Roger that. Want us to meet you there. Take sailor off your hands? … over."

"Roger that … over."

"Roger. Will wait for you there … over."

"Estimate ETA … one hour … over."

"Roger … over and out."

• • •

Ronde Island was a helluva lot smaller than she hoped it would be. There were a couple of hills in the middle and with the skies clearing, she could see both ends of it. As they got closer, she could see two big rocks – he said they were named, 'The Sisters' – and it looked like they were heading right for them. Then, as the sun broke through, she watched her Ahab maneuver Deckadence around the outcrops and into the most tranquil, idyllic bay she'd ever seen. The turquoise water was brilliant, and she could see the sandy bottom even though the depth-meter registered forty-four feet. The coast guard launch was already at anchor.

He said, "We'll drop anchor and let them come to us."

In about ten minutes the coast guard zodiac pulled alongside. "Permission to come aboard?"

A smile crossed his face, the first she'd seen in what felt like an eternity and it not only exuded happiness, it was filled with relief. He explained to the coast guard that JK and his two henchmen had been chasing them and were dangerous characters.

A very weak JK said, "Yale, if I might." He pulled him aside. "You and the woman saved my life. I will be forever indebted. There is no need to tell anyone. I will cease and desist all actions to stop the acquisition and sign all shares over to you as soon as I'm back in New York. No conditions. And I'll deal with the Somalians, you need not worry."

"And Zofia?"

"She's free to do whatever she wants. I'll take no action against her."

Victoria asked, "What guarantees do we have?"

Although JK's body was pale and exhausted, there was no weakness in his eyes. "A man's word … trust."

She smirked. "I've heard that before."

Yale touched her arm. "Actually Hon, this is one-time trust might be okay. I've known this man for quite sometime and despite his reputation, he's Polish, working class. That means a man's word is his bond." He turned to JK. "Right?"

JK nodded and murmured, "Right."

She looked at JK. "Keep in mind, your entanglement with Somalia is just a matter of a phone call to the State Department and FBI."

"You have my word. Your secret is safe with me." Then he shook her hand. "You too ma'am." He was taken to the coast guard launch and ten minutes later they disappeared around the head of the island. She hoped it was closure. But wondered what trust really meant to someone like JK. Would they ever be safe?

CHAPTER FIFTEEN

After swimming naked in the warm waters of the secluded inlet, they showered, changed and curled up together in the cockpit, sipping chardonnay in the soothing sun. And then she began to sob. Softly at first and then uncontrollably. The tighter he held her the more her meltdown, and with every kiss on the top of her head, she burrowed deeper into his chest. He was her silent giant, her real-life Ahab.

There was nothing to say. Words could not wash away the feelings. He welcomed her tears, knew they were necessary. They'd experienced, in just a few hours, both sides of life, from glorious love-making and the eruption of life among the whales to the near-disastrous edge of death. He'd never really been afraid – there'd been no time or place for that – but he knew the danger. Despite his confidence, tropical storms were unpredictable, and Victoria's presence had magnified everything. The fact that she was inexperienced, and he'd put her at risk, was unacceptable. He had not allowed for the unexpected change in weather – ignoring a first-principle of sailing. In his passion to be with her, and for the adventure of a day on the high seas, he'd ignored a possible shift in weather. He only had himself to blame. And he'd foolishly underestimated JK, assuming he would leave the island, never thinking he'd attempt to create 'an accident' at sea. Diabolical. And ironical that JK was almost the victim.

Her tears subsided, and they slid down onto the long seat, lying arm in arm, legs entwined. If not for their exhaustion, they would have celebrated their conquering of the sea and beating the bad guys with the mutual conquest of their bodies and souls. Instead, they dozed off.

She stirred first, then he groaned and stretched his long legs into the air. "Freedom is looking at your bare feet against a tropical blue sky with your love at your side."

She shifted her legs and raised them skyward between his. "No, freedom is looking at your bare feet between the bare feet of your lover, both pointing high into the tropical sky."

He chuckled. "I'd rather be looking down at you instead of up at my feet."

"I'd like to be looking up at you *and* my feet."

"That can be arranged."

"And just how do you propose to do that on these skinny seats?"

He stood, pulled her up, picked up the long cushion, led her to the foredeck and dropped the cushion. "It is sailing custom for the first-mate to lie on the foredeck, point her bare feet toward the sky, in a north-northeasterly direction and scan the sky for anything that the captain should be aware of. And notify him of anything she sees."

He stood over her, his shadow shading her from the sun. She said, "I see a storm brewing. Big. Strong, Hot. Turbulent. Ferocious …" She grabbed his arm and yanked him down. After that she remembered nothing. Other than she was in paradise.

After recuperating and jumping in the water to cool off, he took out his mobile phone. A signal was available. "First things first." He called the marina and informed them that they would not be back until tomorrow. Then he called the Pentagon people and let them know that his pilot would be in touch and they would be flown back to Washington as planned and he and Victoria would follow the next day. She called Carl Kennor and brought him up to date – not all the details – and assured him Kondracki had agreed to everything. And then they did what two people in love, alone on a deserted, tropical island, do. Made indelible memories.

He was a strong swimmer and decided it would be fun if they swam across the inlet, which was about a hundred yards. He was standing at the bow in his bathing suit. "Hey, let's swim over there," he shouted, as if challenging her to a race.

She was a good swimmer but was not about to cross the bay. "No way." She pointed into the beach. "Let's swim to shore and walk the beach."

"Nah. Com'on. You are a good swimmer, right?"

He looked irresistible in his Speedo, like an Olympic swimmer. "I could beat you any day but – "

"So put your money where your mouth is Ms. investment banker … how much if – "

"I've got four-hundred-million. How much you got smart-ass … actually, nice-ass?"

"I'll beat you by ten-lengths."

"It ain't you I'm worried about beating …" She nodded out toward the ocean. "It's the shark."

"You're kidding. There ain't no sharks in – "

"I saw Jaws. And I ain't going back in the water to swim that far."

He came back to the cockpit and put his arms around her shoulders. "Is my beautiful, tough-as-nails, investment partner a fraidy-cat? For someone who handles Wall Street sharks with ease, what's a couple of Reef sharks? I'll take care of you, promise."

"With a body like yours, you probably could wrestle Jaws to a draw." She ran her hand across his sunbaked chest. "But I don't want any scratches on this magnificent specimen, unless they come from these." She lightly dug her nails into his skin.

"I suspect you're about to bring out the handcuffs."

"I forgot them." Then she pushed away, turned and dove into the water and was heading for the beach before he reacted.

For a moment, he stood on the deck admiring her lithe body stroking through the water. "Four-hundred-million says I beat you to the beach." He dove in.

Just before the water got shallow enough to touch bottom she felt a hard tug on her leg. For an instant, panic – the automatic Jaws reaction. Then he pulled her back, grabbed her waist and tossed her up in the air. She was laughing deliriously as she fell into the water.

He was grinning like a boy who had just won a high school swim meet. "I win, I win … pay up."

She wiped the salt water from her face and reminded herself that this was not a dream. There, against a backdrop of spectacular sea and sand, stood her man, her Ahab, her investment partner, her sexual paradise … her everything. He moved through the water toward her, two powerful arms lifted her against his mountain of a chest and he kissed her long, deep and wet. She never wanted to leave this moment, this island, ever.

He took her hand. "Let's explore."

As they walked hand in hand, she was aware that there was just the beach and them. No one else. The coast guard had said nobody lived on the island and the only people who came were the odd fishermen or overnight sailors. "This must be what it was like for Robinson Crusoe?"

"That would mean you're my female version of his guy Friday … but a lot more beautiful."

"Who owns this island?"

"If you're my Friday, then every day will be my TGIF."

They walked and hiked and climbed to the top of one of the hills and sat there for the longest time, soaking in the splendor.

He said, "We should build a home right here."

"What about over there? Looking more south."

"Great panorama." He pointed to the bay where their boat was. "And we could build a sturdy pier down there for Deckadence. And maybe a power boat for quick runs to Grenada for food and water." He hugged her. "I wouldn't need anything else … food, water and you."

"I'm serious."

"I hear ya' ..." His thoughts drifted.

She asked. "Do I hear a but?"

He scrunched her closer. They were sweaty, it was hot. It was wonderful. But amid the beautiful visions in his mind there were clouds. Not storm clouds but clouds he had to clear up before he could turn any fantasy into reality. He couldn't promise her anything until she knew everything. And that was on him. It was a responsibility he had to face sooner or later, and sooner was better. If he could. "Let's head back."

She let his silence go and took his hand as they headed down the hill. She didn't want this moment to be disrupted, there'd be a time and place for unanswered questions and untold secrets.

Back on the beach, gazing out at their boat, it looked further than she remembered. Perhaps it was because she was tired from the sun and exercise. As if sensing her feelings, he put his hand in the small of her back and eased her into the water.

"We're both tired so we'll swim out slowly. It's only fifty yards. The waves are crashing a bit so as soon as it drops off let's dive over them. And stick together."

She knew it was more than fifty yards but loved his reassurance and gentle strength. They dove in and swimming next to him, his arm constantly touching her, she had no thoughts of tiredness or Jaws.

Later in the afternoon a fisherman came along the beach with a large sack over his shoulder. He stopped and waved and then held up a huge lobster from the sack.

Yale yelled. "How much?"

She couldn't make out the reply but before she knew it he dove in, made a deal and was back with a live, four-pound lobster.

He insisted she sit and take in the sunset while he prepared dinner. The roll of the boat made him look even more athletic as he moved about starting the barbeque, boiling water and pouring wine. If she wasn't so tired from hiking, she would have munched on him as an appetizer. Instead she watched the sky being painted in grand hues of red, pink and purple, as the sun set over the sea, the same sea that almost ended her dreams. After the most sumptuous lobster dinner she'd ever had – better than the finest restaurants in New York or San Francisco – and drinking more than she should of his favorite Chardonnay, they curled up together, his arms and legs enveloping her every emotion. The next thing she remembered was being carried below and laid on the bed. She felt the flowing heat from his kiss and slipped into the Caribbean night.

. . .

She woke out of a dream – waves washing over her – and then realized it was only the sound of the waves lapping against the boat as it undulated gently in the breeze. She was safe, curled tightly in his embrace, forming the perfect spoon. His breathing, her breathing, the waves, were in harmony. She didn't want to lose the moment, so she stayed perfectly still and let her mind trace the length of her body making sure every inch was touching him. One foot was slightly away from his leg, so she gingerly moved it. When it touched, he stirred. And pressed against her. She stirred. He stirred … and then his arms tightened around her. She pressed into him. He stirred again. She pressed more. His heat rose. Her skin went buttery. The rise and fall of the waves and the rippling of his body seemed one and the same and he reshaped the spoon without ever releasing her. Her head turned on the pillow, he took her mouth, his thick legs moved across hers, never losing contact, never relinquishing control. His force was erotic. Her legs welcomed his heavy, hot, hard body between them. There was no room to move and the rise and fall of the boat magnified the closeness. Instinctively, she lifted her legs and her feet touched the ceiling of the cabin. The strength she felt, the force she got when pushing her feet on the ceiling was intoxicating. She had him.

He felt her lift. He was in the grip of her long, supple legs. He arched and pushed. She lifted and pushed. He pushed. She lifted.

His weight was demanding. Heavy. Unyielding. It triggered an inner strength in her, a need to control, a need to never let him go. She forced her feet hard into the ceiling, tightened her legs around him, determined to lift him to the height of ecstasy.

He gave into being trapped, accepted his vulnerability. He wanted to be whatever she wanted. She lifted. He gave. She demanded. He gave. She was not only in paradise, paradise was in her. She took all of him. He relinquished everything.

After a breakfast of mouth-watering lobster omelets – being a great cook was one more thing she loved about him – they set sail for St. George's. The winds were steady and the sky cloudless. Even with one sail, he said they'd be back by noon. She soaked everything in – the sun, the breeze, her hero, her future. What the future held was anybody's guess but she was guessing – hoping – it would be fabulous. They'd consummated their love, and the biggest acquisition of her career would be consummated within a week and she'd be a helluva lot richer. She calculated Yale would be worth over a billion. But the money didn't matter, this was now for love, not money.

As the sea spray tingled on her face and made a mess of her hair, her dreams drifted over the ocean. What would they do? What would it be like working with him, overseeing Xcryption? She'd represent Kennor Capital's four-hundred-million and collect her multi-million-dollar bonus. And what would he do? What did he want? She watched him handling the boat as if he was seducing a woman. He sure as hell had seduced her. Willingly. Completely. The seduction was total. The conflict of interest resolved – well, almost. She'd never been here before, never all in. *Was he all in*? Her heart said yes. Her body said yes. Her mind asked, *what was he hiding*? She would ask him on the plane. Why spoil these last hours in paradise?

The 15-knot breeze was easy sailing and he enjoyed the relaxation, basking in the magnificence of the sun and the sea. It didn't matter to him where he was, where he was going, or how long it took to get there, it was the journey that counted. For him sailing was a metaphor for life. Take it on as it's served up – navigate, adapt and change course as required. The only imperative was survival. And now, his metaphor had an added piece, love. Victoria. Although she was seated against the mast, high on the port side, twenty-five feet away, he felt every inch, every ounce, every hope in her. His hope. Her hope … their hope. As he sailed into the next chapter of his life with her, he had one last thing to do. He had to prepare her for what might lie ahead. But not now, not in the middle of paradise. He'd talk to her after the Pentagon deal closed. They'd have a celebratory dinner at his favorite Washington restaurant.

CHAPTER SIXTEEN

She was exhausted by the time they were in the limo heading for the airport. She was ready for a nap after the glorious return sail and packing – she'd wrapped the handcuffs in the red Teddy with a knowing smile – but she must get him to open up on the plane. She'd drink lots of coffee and no wine.

She was on her second glass of Chardonnay and hadn't summoned the willpower to spoil the high they were enjoying, laughing and reminiscing. And every time he touched her she had no interest in anything else. She'd wait for an opportunity to segue into her questions. And then it was there.

He said. "So after the Pentagon signs on Wednesday and the money is in the bank, what are we going to do? There'll be some loose ends to tie up and paperwork, but hell, we gotta celebrate, right?"

"For sure … speaking of loose ends … shouldn't we … wouldn't it be … wouldn't you like to … clear up a couple of things. I think if – "

"Geez … not now. After the signing … I've got it planned for dinner Wednesday night. Honest. Everything. Promise …" He leaned in, put a reassuring hand on her thigh – the one that had saved her life, and JK's – and with a big grin said, "Trust me."

She laughed. She was caught between the nagging need to know the truth and the desire to prolong their unbridled joy. "I trust you. You know that now. My life was, and is, in your hands. Just need you to reciprocate … and trust me. Trust me with whatever it is you haven't told me. After all, if you can – "

"I can't. Not just yet. It's not about trust, it's about timing. Wednesday night, okay. Now is not good. If I tell – "

"Yale, how can I buy that?" So far, it's never been the right time. You keep pushing it off. How do I know Wednesday won't become Thursday … then next week, and – "

"I get your frustration, I get – "

"It's not frustration, it's responsibility. If this has anything to do with the deal, then I have a responsibility, a fiduciary responsibility to know how it might affect the business and if – "

"That's precisely why I can't tell you – yet. I will tell you, and your responsibility will be fulfilled. But not yet, not until – "

"Until hell freezes over?" She felt the words slip between her lips. It was more a harsh whisper than a yell, but she regretted it the second it was out.

He got up and walked to the rear of the cabin. *She's right. And I'm right. Why do two rights have to come between two lovers at such a crucial time? Who ever said, 'timing is everything,' knew what the fuck they were talking about.* He walked back and stood next to her. She'd turned from staring out at the emptiness.

"I'm sorry," he said.

"Me too … but …" She waited for the ache to slide from her heart. "I think we're at an impasse. It's business, not personal. It's about the necessary, not the pleasant. It's not about you and me, it's about Kennor and Apogee. It's about a half-billion-dollar acquisition." She fought to keep from blinking.

He was about to try and convince her to wait until the Pentagon signed but that was before she drew a red line. "Victoria, this is not a time for brinkmanship, we have to be very careful. This deal is not closed and anything I might tell you now, here, today, could jeopardize everything. After the Pentagon, not a problem … well, not as much of a problem."

"What the hell does that mean?"

"Just forty-eight hours. That's all. Is it too much to ask?" He had to get her to agree, even if he couldn't get her to see it.

She asked. "So even after Wednesday's signing, there's another problem? Another secret?"

His brow furled but the warmth in his eyes deepened, trying to reach past her tough outer shell. "In forty-eight hours there will be no secrets, absolutely none between us. Right now, there is one thing that I must protect you from." He paused, eyes unwavering. "Forty-eight hours is worth half-a-billion … and you're worth a helluva lot more than that to me … so, know I am doing this for you, for us. If – "

"How can a secret – living a lie – even for forty-eight hours, be good for us? Nothing undermines love quicker than lies." As she mentioned love she felt a softness return, a smidgen of tension escaped her body. She touched his knee.

He said, "Forgive me for saying this …" He smiled at the corner of his mouth. "Trust me."

Her smile was instinctive. Driven by trust, not by a knowing. By a muscle memory of everything she felt about this man. *I've already trusted him with my life, what's another couple of days?*

He placed his hand on hers.

Calm assurance seeped into her heart. It was as if the necessary, useful and pleasant were all in that moment, all she needed. She nodded, "I trust you."

They kissed and hugged. It was a bit like a high school make up, as the stupid voice in her head rattled on, *Is that it? Did I just give into him, again? Am I really such a wimp to his charm. Stop it Dyson, it's the right thing to do. Yeah, but how do I go from being a tough-ass bitch to a little kitten, in seconds? Has love robbed me of all control, of all the self-discipline I spent years working on?*

They talked and touched the usual amount – well, maybe not quite as much. She rationalized it as exhaustion but her female instincts said something was a little off, they weren't a hundred percent. His secret was casting a shadow. She knew it, he knew it.

It was early evening when they landed in New York and they'd agreed that she should go to her condo and he to his because they had a jam-packed day tomorrow, before flying to Washington on Wednesday. He said lightly, "It'll be a test to see if we can stand being apart for twelve hours."

She didn't need a test to know she'd hate every minute of it but figured he also wanted some relief from constantly facing the secret elephant in the room. Less tension was probably a good thing.

She entered her apartment, parked her suitcase in the bedroom and as a hollow feeling crept over her, she craved peanut butter but didn't have the energy to go to the kitchen. She flopped on the bed and curled into the fetal position, pillow between her legs. She had one thought, *this is going to wrinkle the shit out of my linen slacks.* But she didn't want to think, she wanted to dream.

• • •

Yale sent a text at six am. 'Morning sunshine … see ya' at 7:15.' She smiled. The flatness lingered. But it had to go. She was no longer in a Caribbean paradise. The reality was a life full of big money, big expectations, big problems. He'd be in go mode, she better be too.

The skirt on her navy-blue, suit was tight, not too tight, just sexy tight, and it sure caught his attention when she slipped into the limo. After a more-than-a-peck kiss, he refocused. "Morning Beautiful. Sleep okay? I tossed and turned half the night thinking about – "

"I cried myself to sleep. It was stupid, I – "

"What – what's that about?"

"Just exhaustion. Release from – "

"Not our drama I hope?" He touched her leg.

"Just need to regroup." She took in his deep brown eyes. "Was one helluva fuckin' week you know … you *were* there, right? It *was* you who saved my life, saved JK's life? That was you who swept – "

"Who fell in love with you? Who shared one helluva fuckin' week with you?"

She kissed him as if they were back on Deckadence. She couldn't stop. Somehow she avoided crawling all over him and rumpling the hell out of the navy-blue suit, although he grabbed her ass so hard the imprint of his hand might still be there when they arrived at the office.

New York was New York and yet, as vibrant and romantic as it was, when they reached Apogee's offices, they were both in go mode. They were greeted with a standing ovation. He whispered, "Guess I shouldn't have emailed Mandy and told her we'd pulled off the deal." He acknowledged everyone with a wave, then raised his hand over her head and pointed down, repeatedly, indicating she was the one who should get the credit. She smiled and quickly wished herself into the confines of his office.

"How embarrassing. Did you plan that?"

"Of course not. That's just who they are." He squeezed her arm. "Mandy probably sent an all-staff email. But that's good. I want them to know how instrumental you have been, and will be, as we ramp up Xcryption." He wanted to kiss her but knew better. Business must remain separate. And there were still problems that had to be taken care of – today. Preparation of the final Pentagon contract, transfer of Zofia's shares and making sure Kondracki was out of their lives.

The whirlwind began, and they went their separate ways. Meetings with half-a-dozen accountants and lawyers; tweaking spreadsheets; a tough call with Carl Kennor and scheduling a three o'clock meeting with him. She and others had several stand-up meetings in Yale's office to brief him on what Kennor and the State Department said, and two awkward calls to Zofia. She was snotty, bordering on nasty. But Victoria didn't give a shit, she was gone. *Sayonara.*

He spent most of the morning reviewing drafts of the Pentagon contract and discussing JK with lawyers, who had arranged for him to officially, in writing, agree to cease and desist. As back up, Yale asked her to have Kennor get compromising information on JK from the State Department. Out of these discussions came JK's admittance that he'd planned to have them be victims of 'an accident at sea.'

He spoke with Victoria several times throughout the day and it was all business. But even when there were three or four other people in the room, he struggled to ignore her presence. She was tantalizing, especially when she was all-business. In charge. In control. In one meeting, just before she left for Kennor Capital, she had a briefcase on a strap over her shoulder and all he could see – imagine – was a tote bag with handcuffs and a red teddy under her navy-blue suit. *She wouldn't wear red under blue? Wonder what color she's wearing?* If they were going to work together, he had to compartmentalize sexual fantasies.

She turned to leave and then paused. "Yale, do you have a minute?"

"Sure."

When the door closed behind the others, she approached his desk. Reaching into her briefcase, she took out a piece of paper and handed it across the desk. Pulling him in with her eyes she spoke in a whisper. "Love you." And turned and walked out.

He didn't reply. Couldn't. The paper was blank. Nothing on it. He sucked in his primal urge as he watched the most perfect, navy-blue ass leaving his office. *Black. Bet she's wearing black underwear.*

• • •

The meeting with Carl Kennor – more like a grilling and admonishment – was brutal. She hated his style of confrontation, but it was a necessity of the job. *Besides, after living through gale-force winds on the high seas, shit, this is a piece of cake. In fact, Carl is a piece of shit*. It helped her listen to his insensitive remarks about her relationship with Yale and how he was drawing a redline in terms of their investment.

"One iota, one hint, of distraction from our financial goals and he's gone. And you're gone. There are strict terms in our shareholders' agreement and for the next year, he's tied into us tighter than a monkey's ass."

You're the monkey's ass. And he's tied to me, not you. Obviously, the next year was important for Yale's financial well-being because he couldn't sell his shares and had to remain CEO of Xcryption for that period. And her bonuses were tied up in Kennor Capital for a year. After Carl's blistering, he agreed to have the State Department ensure Kondracki was out of the picture for good.

It was after six when she got back to her desk. The place was still half-full of staff and Yale was in the board room with Mandy and a dozen people. Around seven, he wandered down to her office. He had a smirk on his face and a piece of paper in his hand. He placed it on her desk.

She looked into his eyes. "Mr. Walters. What can I do for you?"

He didn't say a word. Just nodded at the paper.

She said nothing.

Finally, he said, "Just returning your note Ms. Dyson?"

She put her hand on the paper but did not pick it up. "Would this be about money … maybe Monopoly money?"

He added. "About going directly to jail, not passing Go, not collecting two-hundred dollars?"

"Jail?" Who is the jailer?"

"Has to be someone with handcuffs. Someone tough. Someone who can take total charge, someone who – "

"Who wants to control everything, who wants to – "

"Exactly."

"Who wants to have fun playing games rather than working?"

She was flushed, hot and getting wet.

"Exactly. And that piece of paper is an application form. Just sign it and you get to be the jailer, and buy Boardwalk, Park Place and all the hotels you want. And …"

She picked up a pen, scrawled her name across the paper and pushed it toward him. She said nothing. Her eyes said everything.

He picked up the paper, folded it, tucked it in his shirt pocket. "Ms. Dyson, you are now officially, the jailer. The limousine leaves in fifteen minutes and it will take you to your new jail." He turned and walked away.

She called after him. "Who are you?"

"Your prisoner."

CHAPTER SEVENTEEN

The morning after was beyond her wildest fantasies and the omelet Yale whipped up was as good as any Michelin chef could create. And despite the fact it was 5:30 AM, they topped off the most glorious night of love-making with Dom Perignon and orange juice.

His brownstone, her jail, was out of some yet-to-be-made movie. It was just off Fifth Avenue, in the Sixties, she hadn't paid attention. Might be on 62nd or maybe 63rd? It was four stories. But there was no second floor. He'd removed it. When she came through the entrance, she gasped. She'd stepped into an atrium and looking up saw an opening in the ceiling, and a small, bird-cage elevator that climbed up the far wall and through the opening to the third and fourth floors. Breathtaking.

Last night she'd been so drunk on love, she didn't remember much, but she did remember the ride up the elevator and every inch of him engulfing her. He'd carried her off the elevator and it was as if from the moment they'd left the first floor, they were on a trip to their very own heaven, going higher and higher, until there was only the two of them. Nobody else. Nothing else.

It wasn't until sometime in the early morning hours when she was shuffling barefoot down the hall that she noticed the handcuffs clipped to the weight bench in his workout room. As she returned to bed, the fog of sexual exhaustion began to recede and she recalled some of the night's details. How light she felt when he carried her off the elevator, and how wet she was. The cool night air as he laid her on a white-whicker lounge on his rooftop terrace.

And protesting that she was supposed to be the jailer, not him. He said something about not passing Go yet. The evening breeze had caressed her nipples and as he slipped her panties off, she slipped into a semi-state of amnesia. She remembered his penetration and the unbelievable power in his body, on top, under, behind and … yes, the clinking of metal, the handcuffs … and her skin sticking to the leather bench. And at least two or three climatic floods.

Her prince charming beamed. "More Dom? Or coffee?"

She nodded no. *Where the hell does he get the energy?*

"Wheels up in forty minutes."

She didn't want to go anywhere. Didn't want to interrupt the remembering. Didn't give a damn about wheels up, she wanted bodies down, in bed. More love. More heaven. More sleep.

At 7:15 they were on their way to Washington. For her, the only blemish on the horizon would be after the Pentagon signing, at their celebratory dinner, when all secrets were to be revealed.

They signed the papers and were back at the hotel by four. He could see the tiredness in her beautiful blues. "Why don't you take a power nap. Reservations are for seven."

She kissed him. "See ya' in an hour handsome."

It was almost six when she woke. He moved the reservation to eight and let her shower alone. If not, he'd be changing the reservation to breakfast.

Absolutely nothing made her knees weaker than her man standing before her in one of his finest, custom-tailored suits. And he always had the perfect tie. Bold, colorful, classic. *To hell with dinner, let's rip that suit off and go for a repeat of last night.* From her dreamy feelings, all she could muster was a quiet, "Wow!"

"I'll double your wow. And bet the house on you." *Where does she get these fabulous dresses?* It's not just the fit, which is mouthwatering, it's the style. They're made for her body, her beauty, here spirit. They become one with her. You notice the dress but it's just a seamless part of her aura, her mesmerizing poise. She exudes a sexual presence and the dress just illuminates it.

She was unaware of the short limo ride and everyone around her. She heard the maître d' say, 'Good evening Mr. Walters,' but she didn't notice him. At the table, there were two dozen stunning, peach colored lilies and a bottle of Dom Perignon on ice. At that moment, the farthest thing from her mind was some unimportant secrets.

After the wine was opened and the waiters faded into the background, he had only three things on his agenda. Joy. Honesty. Love. The joy had begun, honesty was next, and love was for the rest of their lives.

Although he'd been constantly touching her and squeezing her hand, she knew this squeeze was different. It was in his eyes.

"This isn't easy. And I am sorry that – "

She squeezed back. "Don't be sorry."

"The reason I couldn't tell you until now, although complicated, it came down to protecting you … having to protect you."

"Me?"

"Because of your responsibility to Kennor Capital and to the integrity of the deal. And your financial well-being. Not to mention your career – "

She squeezed his hand again. "Is this about money. Because I don't give a damn about the money when it comes to – "

"Yes … And no … Both."

"If this is about you and me … then I am all in." She pulled on the hesitation in his eyes. "I trust you."

"It's some of both. At first it was about money. Then our love came along. But by then the money was in the way, so to speak, I had – "

"So to speak? How?"

"This deal depended on me. Without me, Kennor Capital would not have the deal. I had to put it together, be out front. Close the Pentagon contract. Deal with JK and Zofia. And commit to running the new company. We all knew that." He went on talking and explaining.

She realized he was rattling on and avoiding the point. She guessed his hesitation came from fear, maybe fear of her reaction, their relationship. "Yale. It's okay. It's me … trust me. Trust us."

"As I said, it's us…. And it's the company, the deal … their connected." He put his other hand on top of theirs. "I have Hodgkin's lymphoma … Hodgkin's disease…."

She saw a slight movement beyond the table, maybe a waiter passing, but everything was frozen. Her mind shut down. Breathing stopped. Her heart collapsed. The word Hodgkin's ripped through her like wildfire, searing her skin, racing into every pore, burning into her emptiness. Her heart leapt into his moment of fear, eyes raced to his. She didn't speak. Just put her other hand on top of his.

He felt the release, the flash of truth flooding the gap between them. He saw her visceral panic. The spiking horror, the plummeting heart, a tear of fear rising behind her blue eyes. He rushed to lift her heart. "It's not that bad … I was diagnosed years ago, treated and I'm good to go. Have been for years. It's the same as the hockey player, Mario Lemieux … hell, his was more than twenty years ago and he came back and played hockey. Mine was ten years ago, I'm perfectly fine. And intend to stay this way until I'm ninety. All of it with you." His smile and radiating warmth were meant to reassure.

She slipped her hand up his thick forearm. *He's far too strong and healthy, he can't be sick? Can't be?*

"The problem isn't the Hodgkin's … it is – was – the Xcryption deal."

Her eyes and jaw dropped. Her lips tried to form the word *what?*

"This is the part that matters – the Hodgkin's is taken care of. But what I've done to hide it is what you and I have to deal with. It's minor, doesn't have to be a big deal. Depends how we handle it." His eyes held hers. "At first, I didn't give it much thought, have done it before, in doing deals. But after I met you, I had second thoughts.

Doubts. I figured you'd uncover it so hid it from you. Then when I admitted to myself how I felt about you, I was concerned about putting you in jeopardy. Then I started – "

"Yale … tell me."

"On my medical disclosure forms between Kennor and Apogee, I didn't disclose the Hodgkin's. It could have killed the deal. I mean … it's gone … and all that. But I thought because of my ongoing responsibility to run Xcryption, it might disqualify me. Full disclosure is a legal issue. Not fully disclosing a serious medical issue is cause to break an agreement … Hodgkin's is cancer. Carl could opt out. And I knew JK could – would – use it against us. And maybe Zofia – they know. And I wanted – "

"The money was my decision, not Carl's. I recommended the deal. I could have recommended it, despite your problem – *if* you'd told me." It was a plea, not a reprimand. She was so intent on the disclosure problem, she'd temporary let go of the heart-breaking news. "I knew you were hiding something, sensed it."

"It was wrong of me. But I didn't want to risk the deal. Especially put you in jeopardy. And I didn't know I was in love with you then."

"And now?"

"I'm telling you … no more secrets." He half-stood, leaned over and kissed her.

It was embarrassingly long for a posh restaurant, but she ate it up. And she would have eaten him up, right there, if she could – maybe fulfill his fantasy of sex in a public place. Reluctantly letting him go, she said, "There's a way of handling this disclosure form omission. It's not the first time someone has forgotten to disclose something. It's a technicality, we'll fix it."

"But you can see my dilemma. If I'd told you before the deal closed it could've put you in jeopardy if you'd decided not to reveal it. And if you revealed it, as your responsibility to Kennor, he might have walked." He shrugged. "And I was afraid JK or Zofia might use it to leverage me. That's one of the reasons I didn't take you to meet him in Grenada. That and your safety."

"Yeah, that was shitty. But they're gone, we're here and the deal is done." Saying it made her feel better.

He lowered his voice. "Are the handcuffs in that bag?"

"What if they were?"

"The men's room here is plush and large. Farthest stall is way over in the corner – "

"An attendant?"

"Twenty bucks is plenty of reason for him to take a ten-minute break." His mouth turned into a mischievous smile. "Trust me."

"Ten minutes?"

"Five."

"I need a lifetime with you … a lifetime of five-minute, five-hour, five-day dalliances. But I ain't being handcuffed in a men's washroom, you're gonna have to take me home. Besides, I didn't bring them."

The restaurant came back into focus and the hedonistic pleasures of gourmet food and fine wine carried them through a joyous evening. He told her all about the Hodgkin's, they talked about the months ahead as they ramped up Xcryption and they estimated how much he'd be worth and what her bonus from Kennor Capital might be. She'd be rich enough to be comfortable for the rest of her life and he'd be on the Forbes 400 list of billionaires. But the money didn't matter, this was love.

The next morning Victoria, once again, couldn't remember it all. It was dream-like amnesia. And again, her incredible lover, the filthy rich CEO of Apogee and Xcryption, had taken her on a magic carpet ride to a heavenly place that was filthy rich in love-making and sexual fantasy. And on the morning after, he was again whipping up gourmet omelets with orange juice and champagne. Then she had a flashback, remembering him dripping champagne on her body and licking it off … her lips, neck, breasts, tummy, vagina ... The champagne was cold, his tongue hot … she heard the clink of handcuffs … he was rough … about then she went over the edge into amnesia.

"More coffee Beautiful?"

"Thanks Handsome." *How much more of everything do I deserve. Is it all too good to be true? It's almost inconceivable.* That word, 'inconceivable,' turned over in her stomach and spiked her memory. There was still one untold truth to be dealt with. Her secret.

•••

As they threw themselves into making Xcryption a success, time flew by. They had announced to Carl Kennor and Apogee employees that they were 'a couple,' and she'd moved into his New York brownstone. He spent a lot of time opening an office in Washington and working with the Pentagon and she went with him when she could. But most of the time he went alone, flying down on Tuesdays, back Fridays. She spent three days a week at Apogee, overseeing Xcryption's finances, recruiting senior staff and looking after the details that her 'boss' hated. But soon it became five days a week and although she still worked for Kennor Capital, responsible for the $400 million investment, she seldom went to Kennor offices. She and Yale were passing ships in the night, crazy busy, but never too busy for a quick hug and a kiss when they could – in private. On one occasion, it was more. After a meeting of a dozen people in his office, she stayed behind for a quick kiss and a squeeze. A quick kiss became a quickie. He tapped on the glass table and asked, "Remember the first glass table?" Her hunger burst. Five minutes later she was coming out of his private washroom straightening her skirt and trying to look all-business. He was retying his tie because she'd almost choked him in her insatiable frenzy.

That evening, as part of their routine when he was in New York, they ate at one of their favorite restaurants, indulging in each other and chatting about their plans.

She mused. "I can't believe we've been running at this pace and how you hold up, spending half your life on a plane. Of course, it's a pretty nice plane and you're a pretty tough guy. But – ."

"Pretty tough? I thought – "

"I meant 'pretty' *and* 'tough.' Pretty, as in handsome. Tough as in sexy rough. And sexy rough as in, if I'd brought the handcuffs, you'd be my prisoner in a cubicle in the men's washroom, right now."

He beamed. "You know my weakness. Don't tempt me."

"Speaking of tough. I think being apart so much is taking its toll. I don't sleep well and going to bed alone and getting up at five does not make Victoria a happy camper."

"That's it. Let's go camping and make wild passionate love high up on a mountain. Let's go to your ski chalet in Taos." He was playing.

"What if I sell the chalet and we buy a condo together in Washington?"

"Don't be silly. You're not selling the chalet. We're going skiing there this winter. And you're not buying a condo. I'm buying a condo ... *our* condo.

Her hands disappeared into the strength of his and his eyes went to her heart.

He said. "This isn't how I planned it. But what the hell…."

Her heart flinched. *What's he talking about? What plan?*

"This is Plan B. Plan A is much more elaborate. Extraordinary. Romantic. Not here." But I'm in go mode, as in go for it. Take the leap. Grab the brass ring ... actually the gold ring ..."

Her heart knew. His eyes said it. His hands said it. His pulse said it. Then he said it.

"Victoria Dyson ... will you marry me?"

CHAPTER EIGHTEEN

As the morning light drifted over the king-size bed – he'd had it custom-made for them – she puzzled over her erotic moments of amnesia. Her mind just seemed to leave her, overwhelmed by emotions. After he'd proposed, she had no idea if she even answered yes. There was little recollection and a ton of sensual overload. There were tears and he kissed them as they ran down her cheeks and she remembered bits and pieces of their love-making and clamping her legs around him, burying her head in his neck and whispering, "I will be your everything, your partner, wife, whore, best friend." Later, as he was dozing, she decided right then and there she would not let another day go by holding onto her secret.

He smelled her before she kissed his shoulder, but he didn't let on. He wanted her to do it again. The pecking at his body, the zapping in his heart, the filling of his life. He opened one eye, rolled onto his back and stared at her beauty. "Morning Ms. Dyson-Walters…. Oh, not yet. But soon."

She felt every ounce of his happiness.

He sensed a grayness in her smile. She was propped up on one elbow.

"Darling Yale." *Get right to it Dyson, Right to it.* "I have a confession, of sorts. I was going to tell you, at some point … but I also didn't tell you because it would've seemed presumptuous … you know, like I was assuming something … that someday we might – "

He lifted his head and kissed her. "As you once said, "Give it to me straight."

"Well … now that we're getting married … before I didn't want you to think I was pushing, I just wanted to …" *Just say it Dyson.* "Every woman's dream is … well, most women … is to … since being a little girl … is one day to get married and have children. For me, the married thing wasn't a big deal and when I cracked the glass ceiling and got into the world of high finance … well, marriage just wasn't in the cards … But you changed all that … and you know, that baby thing just never goes away and …" *Geez, Dyson, get to it.* "But for me … it was not to be – "

He whispered. "Victoria?"

"I can't have children."

Again, he was kissing tears. He tried to wrap all her vulnerability into one big, long, bear hug. He tried to make the two of them one. As the crying receded he kissed the side of her head and whispered. "I don't want children."

Her first realization was how wet his chest was from her tears. But his words were indelible … *he doesn't want children.* He released her from his hug and she furiously kissed his chest, his cheeks, forehead, eyes and then one quick peck on the lips. She didn't dare linger or they'd be lost again, and she needed to explain herself. After all, she was the one who'd made such a damn fuss over trust and truth. She was the hypocrite. She looked at the clock. "It's early, let's make some coffee. I want to explain myself … and apologize."

"There's nothing to apologize for. Nothing to explain. Nothing has changed … who knows, by the time we've had a coffee, I might love you even more than I do now. Twice as much … if that's possible."

"I have to. You beautiful understanding hunk of a man." She told him how she'd had endometriosis and had been infertile for years. She'd had laparoscopy surgery and there was now little to no pain.

He said, "I know."

"You know what?"

"The surgery."

"What?"

"I've explored every inch of you and I saw the small incision near your sexy belly button … I wondered. Suspected. And didn't give a damn."

"Oh my god … how stupid of me." *How could he not have noticed?*

He picked her up off the kitchen stool, wrapped his arms around her bottom, spun her around. "The rest of our lives are hereby dedicated to us, just you and me. We've come a long way baby and we have a long way to go." He put her back on the stool. "Now here's the plan. Plan A. It's your birthday in two days and we're celebrating in Washington. And we're going to go shopping for a new home in Georgetown. And maybe a few other surprises."

"What? What?" She jumped up and down like a teenager on her sixteenth birthday.

"You have to wait." He kissed her with a kiss that just might carry her through the anxiety of not knowing for two days.

• • •

The evening in Washington was fabulous and they dined in a private room at their favorite restaurant. Typical of him, after dinner he had the waiter bring out a very large box and set it on the floor next to their table. It was adorned with a peach ribbon and bow. His smile filled her with anticipation.

"Happy birthday Beautiful."

She wrinkled her nose quizzically, shrugged, and opened the box. It was full of eight or ten presents.

He smiled. "Memories."

She gingerly opened the first one.

He said, "Rip it."

She did. It was a magnificent photograph, enlarged to about three-feet by five-feet, of the sweeping beach on the Isle de Ronde. "Oh my god …" There were six more, all of the island, all breathtaking. There was the view from the hill where they thought a house could be built. A shot of Deckadence anchored in the bay. And a picture of a lush grassy area under a statuesque coconut tree.

He pointed to the tree. "That's where we're going to be married."

She couldn't speak so just kissed him. The only thing that stopped the heat of the kiss from spiraling out of control was the thought that the waiter was outside the door. *Although he does like tables and public places….*

"My romantic, wild and crazy man. Going back to Ronde. Getting married there. Wow!" She kissed him. "We'll hang some here and some in New York. As constant reminders of our paradise." She lightly ran the back of her fingers across his cheek, stopping on his lips. The need to hold him, forever, was overwhelming. "Any date set yet?"

"Up to you Precious."

"Tomorrow?"

"Wheels up at nine?"

"Too early. I'll still have you in handcuffs."

"Okay. How 'bout a week Saturday?"

"That soon? Don't you have to book the sailboat? Make reservations?"

"No reservations – our life is going to be without reservations."

"Seriously Handsome. When would we go? For how long?"

"Forever."

"When?"

"Forever."

"Uh …"

"You asked how long. I'm telling you, forever."

He was playing but she was confused.

He said. "Since we're getting married there and marriage is forever … until death do us part … we're going to stay, forever …

on our island."

"Yes, yes. Our island. Where our love was beautifully – "

"*Our* island."

She stopped. His eyes said everything – just like the first time she'd met him. Every erogenous nerve-ending in her being burst into ecstasy. In that moment, she knew.

"Victoria Dyson-Walters … Happy birthday. I bought the island … for you."